Dr. Mind

and the Biracial Misfit Part I

Andrew Harris, MA, LPCC, ADDC

The work contained herein has been produced with the intent to provide relevant knowledge and information on the topic described in the title for entertainment purposes only. While the author has gone to every extent to furnish up to date and true information, no claims can be made as to its accuracy or validity as the author has made no claims to be an expert on this topic. Notwithstanding, the reader is asked to do their own research and consult any subject matter experts they deem necessary to ensure the quality and accuracy of the material presented herein.

The data, depictions, events, descriptions and all other information forthwith are considered to be true, fair and accurate unless the work is

Table of Contents

Introduction

Congratulations on purchasing *Dr. Mind and the Biracial Misfit Part I*, and thank you for doing so.

The following chapters will take you into Drew's world. Drew is a biracial young man struggling to fit in at his all-white school. He works to connect with those around him and is a constant victim of discrimination based on the color of his skin, his weight, and his social standing. Drew also faces a harsh reality and struggles deeply with his racial identity in his community. He feels like an outsider looking in, but when Drew and his family move into the city from his suburban neighborhood, he has hopes that being in a school where his peers look more diverse will be easier. Desperate to fit in, Drew tries making new friends but finds that he has less in common with this new community than he thought he might. Drew encounters a strong pushback from his classmates for seeming entitled and spoiled. He is an outcast in his new school for being different and targeted for not being "black enough." We find Drew at a crossroads and follow him into deep despair. His parents refuse to validate the reality Drew is facing; his brother is unable to help convince them of Drew's struggle. With nowhere to turn and nobody to listen to him, Drew finds himself in a steep downward spiral.

He sees only one way out.

Chapter 1: Drew's World

I look down at the backs of my hands sitting flat on my desk and see something different than everyone else around me. I never thought my life would turn out the way it has so far—a black kid in an all-white school. I've read about the fight for Civil Rights, the segregation in schools in the fifties and sixties, and the struggles people like me have dealt with their whole lives. There is some part of that history that still exists as a reality for me every day. My parents, brother, and I have lived in a rural part of St. Louis since I was born. There are not a lot of people like us in our community. My brother is a year older than me and a grade above me. We attend a public school in the city's suburbs, made up of almost entirely white kids. My brother, myself, and a few others are in the minority, and it's hard not to feel like it every day. Shawn, my brother, made the right moves in his high school career and joined the football team last year, so he has it a little easier than I do. The team and the school can see past his skin color just because he's athletic and hangs out with the right crowd. I am not like him. I'm not like anybody.

I do alright in school; I don't like being there. I'm not popular in school like Shawn. I stay as quiet as possible to avoid being noticed by anyone, and some days it works. Some days I'm ridiculed for being the only black kid in the school, and some days I'm laughed at when one of the guys calls me fat. Either way, the days go by with my head tucked into my sketchbook. Art is my escape, passion, and the one thing that gets me through life at school. The last two hours of the day I spend in my elective art classes. It is smooth sailing compared to the rest of my classes every day. Mr. Pierce makes me feel valued in those two hours. I would spend the entire day there if I could. My last two classes with Mr. Pierce is the most enjoyable part of my day. Nobody is there to bother me, nobody to make fun of the way I look or how quiet I am. I just get to be myself and enjoy it as time goes by. Pierce lets me have the supplies for just about any project I want to try to do, whether it's a wall-size canvas to paint on or some clay to sculpt.

Mr. Pierce's class is a paradise for me. I doubled up on art classes this semester so I could spend two hours a day there. Pierce is a great guy. He's been my art teacher since sixth grade. He's the only teacher in this entire school that truly understands me, let alone defend me. The football team's bullies give me a lot of shit in most of my other classes, but Pierce never lets anyone talk down to me in his classes, so nobody tries it anymore. Pierce says I'm a stellar artist and tries to help me be the best I can be, unlike many of these teachers. I'm mostly ignored by them or thought of as a troublemaker simply because I get in many fights. I used to get sent to the office a few times a week because one of the football guys would say something clever, and I would stand up for myself. They'd be pegged as the innocent ones while I had to make the trip to the principal's office. Everyone loves the guys on the football team, especially the teachers. Teachers adore the football team in this school, and I'm just a freak. It's no coincidence that I'm the only black kid in a sea of white people. The last fight I got in was with the captain of the football team, Jake. He said something about my family being poor and my dad being a degenerate because he's black. I lunged at him, but three of the other football guys in the class pulled me off of him. They held me down, and Jake got on top of me and pulled his fist back to hit me. Before he made contact, the teacher broke it up, sent them to their seats, and, surprise, sent me to the principal's office.

That fight with Jake encouraged the school to put me on a plan. Well, that paired with my skipping school more than eight days each month. In my defense, I couldn't help but not want to attend when I had to deal with being bullied at least once every day. Part of the plan they put me on was that if I got into one more "altercation" with anyone for the rest of the school year, I'd face expulsion. If I had it my way, I'd prefer not to go to school anymore, but my parents have different feelings on the subject. I have to sit back and take everything that comes my way now. I've trained myself not to fight back, not to get angry, and not to start anything with those guys even when I feel compelled to fight. I don't speak in class unless a teacher asks me a question. I've resolved myself to not speaking to any of my classmates either. I don't want any unnecessary attention put on me by anyone. My goal since the fight is to remain as quiet and out of the way as possible. Then, when the semester is over, I can move on. Jake and most of his friends will have graduated, and I can finally be left alone every day.

Waking up each day is getting more brutal than the last. Dread sets in just knowing that I have to walk through my high school doors and deal with what I know is coming.

I put it off as long as possible every morning. My mom works two jobs so we can make ends meet. She leaves every morning before sunrise and doesn't get home until after dinner. Dad works nights at the factory, so we rarely see him unless it's the weekend. Shawn and I are pretty much on our own. We get up, get ready, and have breakfast all on our own. Shawn is always up before I am. I just can't stand getting up for school anymore. Shawn bursts into my room for the fourth time and slaps the light switch on, knowing full well that I will jump out of bed just to turn it back off. My hand meets his on the light switch this time, and I know the game is over.

"You have to get out of bed and get ready for school, Drew."

"I know," I say, deflated. Shawn can tell I am never fully interested in going, but he never asks why. I can't help thinking that it's just because he doesn't care. Shawn is the favorite child between us. My parents never hesitate to make it obvious, either. He gets better grades than I do, and he's athletic. Shawn gives my parents hope that they will have a successful child, but I am passionate about art, something they don't see as a career. They would prefer I become a doctor or an athlete like Shawn, but neither option is my style. If I could not create for a living, I would never have a chance at being happy or prosperous.

Shawn leaves the room, and I throw on the first shirt and pair of jeans that I can find. I grabbed my backpack, the few dollars that I saved from mowing lawns last week, so I don't have to eat whatever sad excuse for a school lunch is on the menu today, and a Dr. Pepper from the refrigerator for breakfast. Shawn and I take the bus to school every morning since our parents aren't around. He got his license last year but hasn't made enough money to buy himself a car. We can occasionally take the family van out on weekends when mom and dad aren't working overtime. I can get my permit this year, but I don't see the point. I'll never make enough money doing jobs around the neighborhood to buy a car. Honestly, I don't want to add another thing that Shawn can do better than me to the list. I know I'd be a terrible driver. Maybe I will just walk to and from school next year. We don't sit anywhere near each other on the bus. Shawn has a few freshman friends that ride with us. I usually snag a seat as far back as I can and put my bag in the middle next to me, so nobody bothers me. Once we leave the bus, I don't see my brother again until after football practice. It gives me more time in the art room, so I don't mind staying the extra hour after school. Our dad picks us up on his way to work and drops us off a few blocks away from the house, so he doesn't have to go "out of his way."

I do mind having to wait for Shawn's football friends to leave before approaching him after school. I take enough bullying from them during my fourth period, and the last thing I want is for one of them to try something without any teachers around to stop them. I've had my fair share of trouble at school, mainly with the football team. Last semester, I got into four different fights, two of them with Shawn's friends. I packed in a few good punches, but I mostly ended up getting sent home to bandage my face while sitting on the floor. I get two-week suspensions each time, but each player was only sent home for the day. I'm on my last warning while they all got simple slaps on the wrist. The principal constantly reminds me that I'm going to get expelled from school with just one more fight. I tried to stand my ground each time and point out that none of the other guys got in trouble, and almost all of them threw the first punch.

I avoid saying bye to Shawn and make my way through the front doors, trying not to be noticed by anyone around me.

It is difficult being the only black kid in this school, aside from my brother. He makes it even more difficult by being as popular as he is. He constantly shows off his new clothes while I wear his hand-me-downs if I don't have the money to buy my clothes of my own. I take a lot of heat for wearing the same outfits at school. I prefer the few hoodies I have instead of the clothes Shawn has to give me. A lot of Shawn's clothes ended up fitting me since he's much taller and built a little bigger. I feel weird wearing someone else's clothes. I want my own. Everyone knows Shawn; therefore, they know me by association. I'm Drew, Shawn's loser brother. I don't care about the clothes or shoes as he does, and I take a lot of crap because of that. The laughs in the hallway are not inconspicuous. You'd have to be brain dead not to put together that they're laughing at me. I can hear the cheerleaders laughing with the football team when I walk past them in the hall, and when I walk into a classroom, everyone turns to look at me like I'm a freak. I genuinely despise being here day in and day out, just waiting for someone to laugh at me or point at me. It has been getting worse as the semesters in high school go on. Freshman year wasn't too bad. I think the seniors bullying me right now were getting tortured by those in the grade above them. I guess it's just my turn now.

The only thing I like in this school is the line of vending machines in the cafeteria and the art department's safety. We usually get in early enough that I can grab a bag of chips from one of the vending machines, another soda, and head down to the art room before anyone gets there. I can stuff my sketchbook in the cabinet behind Mr. Pierce's desk, so nobody messes with it. None of the teachers make me feel like I fit in as he does. Even if nobody in the two classes I have with him talks to me, he's always there to listen and give me constructive feedback on my work. I have a minute to listen to his ideas for his latest project before I must run back up the stairs to my first period, English. I wait until just before the bell is about to ring before making the trek to my first class to avoid most of the people in the hall. All I have to do is get through the first four periods, then fifth and sixth are a breath of fresh air, well, a breath of fresh paint and pastels, but still fresh, nonetheless. I have been able to make the few friends I have in school in my art classes. Many of us experience the same bullying in school, but I seem to stand out for obvious reasons.

"See you, D," Mr. Pierce always shouts as I push my way through the doors of his class and take the first steps of the day, counting down until I can make it back. I threw the hood of my sweatshirt up routinely and bound up the steps to the school's main level, past the rows of lockers and a left down the hall—room 107. Room 107 is my dull English class. I can barely stay awake in this class, let alone pay attention to what we're reading.

"Made it," I whisper to myself, almost sighing in relief loud enough for the entire class to hear. We got to pick our assigned seats on the first day; naturally, I chose the room's back corner. Nobody ever occupied the seat next to me. English class lets me put my brain on autopilot. I study, I can write decently, and the teacher never calls on me. My brain can focus on how I can get to lunch and go unnoticed through the rest of my day. We are reading Shakespeare today. Surprise, another old white guy. We are constantly reading about something to do with white people or European history, never black history. I blurted out my feelings on this topic one week in class, and I got sent (again) to the principal's office. I guess none of these teachers like it when a black man is complaining about learning white culture, though any black representation in our curriculum is missing. At least reading Shakespeare gives me time to make a rough draft of the piece I want to start working on for my art portfolio. We've read something from Shakespeare every year since I've been in middle school, so I grab my extra sketchbook from my backpack and get to work. The swipe of lead on paper is a relaxing sound, much better than the words of Macbeth. I feel a confident focus when drawing; a rare feeling for me, but it is exhilarating. The minutes on the clock seem to fly by at the speed of light. Every line is a distraction, and before I know it, I realize that I've tuned out the bell to dismiss class.

My lunch hour is after the first and second periods, another highlight of the day. The only thing that gives me the same focus and comfort as art is eating. School, in general, is a significant stress factor in my life, and I don't have anyone to talk to about it. Shawn is busy with his football friends, my parents are either working or ignoring me, and I don't have any friends close enough to understand me. What I have is an outlet, something that has never let me down or made fun of me for the way I am. I have always had food. Eating makes me feel better, more comfortable, and at ease. I cannot explain or control it, but any inconvenience can trigger the desire to eat. If I feel anxious or uncomfortable in a situation, if I get bored, or especially if I have had to deal with one of Shawn's friends making fun of me, I'll feel myself craving something to eat just to take the edge off. Our parents are almost always busy working long hours, so Shawn and I usually grab something from a drive-through on the way home unless our mom plans to order pizza for dinner. As a family, we have always had the means to have whatever food we ask for, and for me, the ultimate comfort is junk food—chips, cookies, pizza, ice cream, you name it. Maybe I've grown accustomed to having something I want; I don't know. I know that it has always been there for me when I needed to escape my reality.

Pepperoni pizza satisfied my craving today, but another trip to the vending machine for a soda was a must before the dreaded fourth period. Thinking about walking into Spanish class fills me with the most unsettling feeling. The school must have enrolled the entire football team in that class with me. Those guys make fun of me more than anyone else in the school, and even though Shawn is friends with all of them, they rarely let up. My fourth class is full of jocks on the team and a couple of the cheerleaders for the team. I always grab a seat as far away from them to avoid the comments and conversations I hear about me. My clothes are not expensive enough; I'm too fat, I'm a creep who draws and doesn't even speak. I have heard it all. I don't even sit with Shawn during our lunch period because he sits with the rest of the football players. He has tried to defend me before, but I think he prefers popularity over our relationship. I can't blame him. If the jocks aren't in the mood to push me around, I can make it through Spanish unscathed, but if they've had a bad day, the torture is relentless.

"Fat kid."

"Why aren't you more like your brother?"

"Do you ever talk? Are your lips too big to speak?"

I just try to keep my head down and take it the best I can without getting upset, but don't think I'm not pissed at the thought of having to do so. If I get into one more altercation with one of these white guys, I face expulsion, then who knows where I'll have to go to school. Mom and dad will probably disown me at that point. The class is only forty-eight minutes, and then the torture is over. I can't complain to any of the teachers because they don't listen, and even if they did, they wouldn't believe a beloved football player over the quiet, weird kid in the corner. If by the grace of God, any of these teachers *did* listen to me and honestly did something about it, the bullying would be ten times worse than it already is. I've resolved to take the harsh words, the laughs, and the jokes for what they are. I'll just keep to myself as long as I can.

Once the torture of my Spanish class has passed, if I can make it down the hallway without running into one of the football goons, I get to be free and be myself in Pierce's class finally. Advanced Application and Drawing & Design are my two final classes of the day, both in the same room and with the best teacher out there. Unlike every other class I have during the day, I sit directly in front to get a good look at how Pierce is applying the pen or brush strokes.

I mimic his every move. He's constantly impressed with the work that I put out in both classes, which is a giant breath of fresh air I've ever taken. It's incredible to be listened to and praised by a teacher in this school, even if it is only for two classes.

We're doing black and white portraits of someone meaningful in our lives this week, something I'm particularly good at executing. This issue for me was choosing the subject matter. Everyone else in the class is doing their mom, dad, or someone else in their family. Don't get me wrong, family is family, and I appreciate mine. They can just be incredibly annoying sometimes. My mom and dad don't listen to me in the slightest, Shawn is off in his little world, and my grandparents live in the city, so we never see them. I don't feel like any of them have been that instrumental in making my life unique that I could choose to draw them for this project, so I make up someone in my mind. Maybe this person would be there when I have questions about homework or what to do when I like a girl. Perhaps they wouldn't be at work so often that I only saw them on Sunday mornings for breakfast. This person might be a brother who sticks up for me when his teammates are trying to beat my face in, or maybe just a friend to be there when I need to talk. Lord knows those kinds of people are in short supply. This person could be the person that's there to help me when I don't have anyone else, but that person doesn't exist. They're just lines on a piece of paper, entirely made up.

Chapter 2: Misfit Makeover

Another morning, another day of being me. Another day to deal with being the "weird kid." I'm struggling more and more every day to keep my head above water. It's almost as if the jocks in school are targeting me, trying to beat me down just for their amusement. I can't take it anymore. I get tormented for being black, cast aside because I'm overweight, and made to feel foreign because of my appearance. What's next? I feel entirely alone in all of this. I have nobody to confide in, Shawn does nothing in my defense at school, but then again, he doesn't see most of what happens. He has to hear about it from them in the locker room after practice or when he's hanging out with his friends between classes.

"Drew, time for school." My mother's arm snakes around the door frame, flipping on the light, but when she sees it's already on, she has to ask me what's wrong. She must have the day off of her cleaning job that wakes her up at four in the morning. She sees my appearance, and as concerned as she can bear to be, she asks, "What's wrong? You don't seem well."

"Nothing. I just feel sick. Headache, stomachache, nauseous. Can I stay home from school today? I already have my assignments for the week." She agrees, somewhat reluctantly it appears. I'm taking full advantage of her being home for the first morning in months. I usually have to call her at work. I've mastered making myself look and sound sick when I don't dare to show my face at school. At least staying home will give me a break from everything happening at school.

Out of the corner of my eye, I saw another figure in the doorway of my bedroom. I was utterly convinced it was my mother coming back to change her mind and send me back into the fire. I was shocked when I saw Shawn standing in my doorway. "Drew, what's up? Can I talk to you?"

"Yeah, I guess. What's going on?" Shawn barely spoke to me regularly, so I can't imagine why he would need to "talk to me."

"Listen, I heard about Jake and the other guys talking about how they were picking on you in one of your classes. If you want me to say something to them or mom and dad, I can."

"No!" I blurted out without thinking. "I'm ok, I-I'll be fine, I mean."

"Ok, cool. I'll see you around, I guess." Shawn sunk out of my door frame, almost like he wanted to say more but didn't know what to say. What is happening? Shawn has never offered to help me in any way, he's never defended me around his friends, and most certainly never offered to talk to our parents about what's happening? How do I know that he'll have my back if I *do* say something?

My eyes meet themselves in the mirror above my dresser, and I stop and think about everything that's wrong with me. Would I have such a hard time if my skin were lighter? Would being more like everyone else in my school solve all of my problems? Maybe if I didn't have acne or built more like Shawn and wore designer clothes and shoes, I'd have an easier time. I bet that if I were a white kid in this school, I'd go unnoticed every single day. The teachers wouldn't target me, and the football team wouldn't come after me. I'd be invisible to everyone. I want that more than anything right now. The reflection looking back at me in my mirror is one of deep sadness and depression. I want to try to fit in with everyone, to try and be more regular. If I can't be a normal kid, I don't want to be me at all. Who would want to be someone like me, anyway? I get made fun of every day for the way I am. Nobody would want this.

I jumped up from my bed and ran down the hall, down the stairs, and out the front door. I had an idea! I burst out the front door just in time to catch Shawn backing out of the driveway to go to school. I knew mom would let him drive the van this morning since she was off for the day. He must've seen me at the very last minute before taking off because when he hit the brakes, the car jolted forward. Now walking, as I was more than out of breath by the time I hit the front door, I approached the driver's side window. I hadn't planned what I wanted to say, and I felt uncomfortable even trying to come up with the words. "What's going on?" My brother had honestly never seen me run before, so I think he knew something was up.

"Jake and the guys in my class make fun of me for the way I dress, my hair even. I don't know what to do, but will you help me be more like you?" I hadn't asked Shawn for anything since we were kids, but I was desperate to do anything I could to get the bullying to stop. "I just have to be at practice at three." I think he sensed the desperation behind my words. This moment is the first time he has ever offered to help me. "Go change, and I'll wait at the end of the street. *Don't* let mom see you."

I ran back to my room just in time to see mom's bedroom door shut. She'd be passed out from exhaustion most of the day, and I knew it. She worked six days a week, at least twelve hours each day. She'd leave before we were up for school and not be home until seven or eight P.M. If she had the chance to be off for a day, she would be totally out of it the entire day, just trying to recover from constant work. I hurriedly threw on yesterday's clothes and grabbed some of the money that I'd been saving in an old jar underneath my bed. I laced up the tattered Converse Chuck Taylor's that

24

I've been wearing since ninth grade and ran back outside. Shawn was waiting at the end of the road just like he said he would be.

I opened the passenger door and climbed in. "You're lucky that mom let me have the van today. She'd flip if she knew we were skipping school to go shop at the mall, so keep your mouth shut."

"We'll be quick. You can drop me off and be at practice by three. I promise." Today is the most we had talked about all year. I was pleasantly surprised. Shawn asked me about what was going on at school on the way to the mall. I finally felt like I had someone to talk to, even though I knew he couldn't do much more than help me try to fit in. Shawn has strived to be popular since we were in middle school. He was the victim of bullying, too, until he started playing sports in school. Being on a sports team is an automatic pass to be popular. It has never been something I cared much about. I'm not athletic enough to be any good at sports.

We pulled into the parking lot of the Riverton Mall. I hopped out and followed my brother inside. "You're going to need shoes." Shawn looked me up and down, "...and pretty much everything else. Let's go." We walked around to what seemed like fifty, maybe sixty stores looking for the right things. The newest Nike shoes, track pants from Adidas, shirts from H&M, all things I would never buy for myself, but I had to trust that Shawn knew better than I did. Over a hundred and fifty dollars, all my savings for the years, and three shopping bags later, we were finally done.

"Can we stop at the food court before we go?" I was starving.

"Drew, that's something else that I need to say to you. You need to look a certain way if you want to take them to take the heat off of you at school. You could eat less, maybe exercise some days. We have a family gym membership. I-I could even help you some mornings before school."

"Yeah, maybe. Thanks." I knew he was right, but what he also said kind of hurt my feelings. I can't help it that eating is a comfort for me, and I've never been one to exercise. I know nobody in that school will take me seriously unless I dress the right way or have money to buy the newest shoes, but I just want someone to be my friend because they like me. At the very least, they could just get to know me and like me for my personality, but I guess that's too much to ask. Does Shawn just think I'm lazy and fat like the guys who make fun of me at school? "Let's just go."

The ride home was a little quieter than the trip there. I was running through our conversation over and over in my head. I know that I'm overweight, and I know that I shouldn't eat as I do, but I can't help how I cope with things? Why should I have to conform to look a certain way just to be treated fairly? Eating is something that brings me the comfort that nobody around me, including myself, can provide. If nobody is there to talk about things with me, I have to get some comfort somehow. That's what eating does for me. Any time that I have to go through something traumatic, I turn to food. What am I supposed to do?

The closer we got to the house, the more Shawn started to push me to talk to our parents about the bullying. "If the clothes and the shoes don't work, and you're still getting made fun of, you need to tell somebody. I can say something to Jake and the other guys, but I can't promise they'll stop. They pretty much run the school, Drew. I don't think they'll take me seriously. You need to talk to mom and dad, the principal, the counselor, or somebody."

"Ok, Shawn, I get it. I'll think about it. You know mom and dad don't listen to me as they do you, and if I talk to someone at school, won't things get worse?"

"Maybe. I-I don't know, but you need to tell somebody, Drew."

I know that I'm right, and somewhere deep down, I think Shawn knew it too. Our parents had always listened to Shawn's problems and catered to his feelings before they even gave me the time of day. He's always been the favorite, the firstborn. Shawn could do no wrong in the eyes of my parents, and that got on my nerves more than anything else. I knew they could listen and care for their children, but why did that stop at Shawn? What was wrong with me that I wasn't deserving of the same treatment as my brother?

The car slowed as we neared the house. Shawn whipped around the middle of the street to drop me off near the front door and make a run to his football practice. It was rare that we got the van for any reason, and I know Shawn didn't want to disappoint mom by using it to help me skip school. I waved goodbye and ran into the house with my bag of new clothes. It turns out Shawn had nothing to worry about; Mom was still entirely out, and Dad hadn't woken up for his night shift at the factory yet. The house was barren and cold, like most days. It seemed like it didn't contain life most of the time. I was by myself almost every day. Our parents were working or asleep, and Shawn was either at practice or shut in his room listening to music. It was just me and my sketchbook all alone. I made myself some of the leftover pizza that was still in the fridge and went to my room to try on my new clothes. The clothes were alright; I just didn't look like myself in them. I didn't feel like myself either. I looked more like Shawn, which could be a good thing, the more I thought about it. I wasn't sure how I could be more confident if I felt less like myself, but I was willing to give just about anything a try at this point.

I sat the clothes and shoes at the foot of my bed for the morning and opened my sketchbook to work on my art project before I went to bed.

I started thinking more about this made-up figure that I was drawing and how much different my life would be if this person were an actual person or if someone in my family could just be a little bit like this person. If either of my parents would listen to me, they might see that I'm genuinely struggling. If Shawn could get away from his ego, he might know that I don't feel like I belong at school, and maybe he could help me try to make some friends. I'm not asking for a lot here; I feel like a little bit of support would go a long way. I'd just like to feel like someone is on my side for a change. Thinking about it triggers my anxiety, and realizing I'm mostly alone in all that I struggle with every day just causes me to want to eat something. Maybe that's a good sign that I should get to bed early. I shoved my sketchbook and pencils back into my bag after getting roughly zero work done and flung myself back onto my pillow. The nights were the most challenging times.

I remember as a child when my mom would come in to tuck me in and read me a story. I know it's childish of me to want some part of that back, but it was indeed a special moment for me each night. When Shawn and I were younger, our parents didn't have to work as much. They both had decent jobs, and we're at home every night. I don't know what happened between then and now. All I know is that back then, I felt cared for and never felt alone. We'd all eat dinner together, something that mom cooked, not a cold piece of pizza warmed partially through in the microwave. After dinner, we'd either watch a movie together or hang out in the backyard and play tag or throw around a baseball. My parents were younger then and probably a bit more carefree. Maybe it's the fact that Shawn and I grew up, started to grow apart, or something else. Life just seemed a bit easier back then. At least I have my bed now, this pizza, and my art to keep me company.

The next day I woke up early, in a good mood, and ready for what I hoped would be a change. I jumped in the shower, took some time to get myself ready, and put on the new clothes and shoes from yesterday's shopping trip. I felt prepared for the day and determined to try to fit in more than I have before. I hope the new clothes and shoes will help give me a little confidence. Maybe I'll finally make a friend.

"Looking good, kid!" Shawn was waiting for me downstairs so we could ride to school together. His words seem to catch the attention of our parents.

"When did you get new clothes?" I temporarily forgot that my mother knew precisely what four outfits I owned and would question if I were wearing something that looked presentable.

"What?" I questioned while running out the front door behind Shawn, who didn't want to get caught in a lie.

We rode to school with less silence than usual between us, and just before the bus parked, Shawn said to me, "Good luck today, man. Let me know how it goes." I was hoping it would go well. I made my way down the aisle and hopped down the few steps exiting the bus.

I noticed that I was walking more confidently on the way from the bus to the school's front doors. I can't say that I've known what confidence felt like before, but I could get used to this feeling. I noticed a few heads turn as I walked down the sidewalk and up to the school's doors. Nobody on the bus seemed to see, but then again, I don't think those people ever notice me. I always sit in the furthest seat to the back and never talk to anyone except Shawn. I entered the school, still unscathed, and stopped for my morning soda at the vending machine just inside the front door. The confidence drained from my body when I saw a group of football guys a few machines down. They noticed me too.

"Look, Shawn's little brother got some new digs. I didn't know they made clothes that big!" The team laughed behind Jake, and I sunk into my shell as he walked closer to me. I thought about turning immediately to run, but I didn't want something else on my record for them to use to make fun of me.

"Where'd you get a shirt that big, huh, buddy?" I noticed his eyes glance down at his hand. There, I noticed an open bottle. The same bottle I was holding. "Isn't Dr. Pepper your favorite? I see you with one in your hand all day, every day."

I didn't have time to respond before abandoning everything to turn around and run. Before I could move, I felt a splash and cold liquid run down the back of my new shirt and another down the back of my pants. This *torture cannot* be happening to me. What did I do to deserve this? I turned around to face them, just to see them all doubled over in laughter. I was standing there in front of everyone while Jake flung out the last drops of soda onto the front of my shirt, completely mortified. It seemed like the entire school had gathered just to laugh at my expense.

"What the hell, guys?" Shawn yelled, to my surprise. He must've come through the front doors just a few minutes behind me, witnessing the entire event. "When are you going to leave him alone?"

"What, Shawn? Do you want some too?" Jake controlled the team, the whole school. Shawn backed down almost immediately, grabbed my arm, and walked me down the hall.

"You have to try to stay away from them, Drew. They're not going to let up."

"Me?! Why do I have to stay away from them? I haven't done anything wrong. I didn't even talk to them. They just attacked me, Shawn!"

"Just stay. Away. I have to go now. Get to class."

I honestly can't believe that he just said that to me. Does he think this is all my fault? He was so cool with everything yesterday. I should've known it was all just a cover. He doesn't care enough to help me truly. I walked straight downstairs to Mr. Pierce's room to beg him to let me stay there for the remainder of the day. There's no way to go to class and face anyone today, not looking like this at least.

The stairs to the art room were at the end of the hall, and I can already tell that with my luck today, Jake or one of his goons will intercept me before I get there. All I could think to do was take off running. I didn't want anyone to see me or laugh at me anymore. The closer I got to the stairs, the more confident I was that the entire football team would pop around the corner at any second.

Three.

Two.

One.

I Made it. I could hear a burst of distant laughter floating down the hallway behind me, so I didn't take a second to stop before hitting the top stair, just a little off-balance. I missed the second stair entirely, hit the third with my thigh, and slid down the other seven until I hit that landing between the two flights of stairs. Everybody at the bottom and everyone at the top decided to stop and turn, not to see if I were ok, but to laugh. I just sat there for a minute, more embarrassed than I've ever been. This day could not possibly get any worse.

Forget the art room. Forget everything today. I picked myself up from the landing and continued down the rest of the stairs, down the hallway past Mr. Pierce's room, and straight out the emergency exit, no doubt sounding the alarm. I don't care anymore. I hate this place with every fiber of my being. I never want to come back. I'll just walk a few miles home from here. It just wasn't worth it to stay and get harassed even further. I picked myself up, gathered my things, and bolted for the door. I ran as fast as I could down the hall, past the art room, and out the school's exit. I ran all the way down the sidewalk and onto the main road. It was just a few miles from here to the safety of my bedroom. I'm done with this day.

My feet pounded the asphalt with every step, but that pain was far less than what I would've felt if I had to stay and face anyone at school again. The steps were grueling; my feet were killing me. What wasn't killing me was the solitude of being around nothing but passing cars, trees, and the occasional dead animal on the side of the road. Being alone is what truly makes me happy. I haven't begun to understand why people are the way they are. Cruel. Hurtful. Even my brother isn't on my side. I don't know where everything went wrong. We used to be so close as kids.

We played outside together almost every day before he got to high school. I remember getting in trouble together for taking our mom's favorite ice cream from the freezer one night after being sent to bed. We snuck into the kitchen as quietly as we could. I grabbed two spoons from the drawer, and Shawn snatched the ice cream because he was the only one tall enough to reach it. We ate the whole gallon in bed with the T.V. on, the volume down. We almost got through the entire rerun of *The Texas Chainsaw Massacre* without screaming and hiding under the blankets. Mom eventually caught us, and we grounded us for nearly two weeks, with no T.V. I miss that Shawn. I miss those days. Everything now is a fog, and we have grown so far apart that we barely speak anymore.

About an hour and a half into my walk, I felt my phone buzz in my pocket. When I pulled it out and saw Shawn's name on the screen, I hit ignore and kept walking. I had nothing to say to him anymore. I'm giving up. Shawn doesn't give up so quickly because he called four more times before I got fed up and answered.

"What?!" I screamed into the phone. "What do you want?"

"Where are you, Drew. Some of the guys told me that they saw you leave school from the emergency doors. I didn't know you were the one that set off the alarm. They're pissed here, you know."

"I don't care, Shawn. Today has been the worst day of my life. You said you would help me. You said you'd talk to them, but you didn't even defend me when you had the chance. Do you think the same things about me that they think?" There was silence on the other end of the line, and the silence was answer enough for me. My phone dropped from my face, and with nothing left inside me, I hit the end button on the call.

Chapter 3: Ball Is Life?

It has been almost a week since Shawn suggested that I talk to our parents about what's happening to me at school, and I still haven't mustered up the courage to do so, mostly because I'm sure that they won't listen. I've had opportunities to tell them, but I can't help but think they'll push aside and treat it like it's not a real problem, not like Shawn's problems; however few there may be. Our mom has always told us we could talk to her about anything, but she's either working late or just emotionally disinterested as we've gotten older. She is the type of parent who always wants the problems fixed without bothering to talk through them. I could come to her with a problem, and the response will always be for me to "fix it." She never wants to hear any details or offer any advice. She just wants the problem gone.

My mom is the first generation in the states. My grandparents immigrated to America from Mexico, hoping to give their family hope for a better future. They taught her Spanish as a child because they didn't know any English. I know my mom has always felt pressure to make their sacrifices mean something, not wasting any opportunity that came her way. Her mother and father were always hard on her. She had to have the best grades, the best job, and work the hardest of her peers. It would make sense that she might have more of a transactional relationship with her mom and then pass that on to her children. I can see she tries to be closer to us. She still speaks primarily Spanish, and she's worked as hard as anyone can so she could support her family, but with two jobs, she barely has time to talk to us. Anytime I bring up something that is bothering me, she talks about how hard she had it and how hard her parents were on her. I've tried to connect with her, but no one ever talks about how hard it is to build a bridge for your parents to communicate to you, especially when you see how much more effortless that connection is with your brother. They celebrate everything Shawn does, or at the very least, takes it seriously. Every win, every accomplishment, every struggle all have my parent's full attention. Hell, I remember when he flunked his biology final; they hired tutors, met with the teacher, and dad stayed up with him till 3 A.M. to make sure he passed. If I ever got below a "B," the most I'd get is a lecture on how I would never be anything.

Our father is an entirely different story. His mother got pregnant with him at sixteen, and her parents kicked her out of the house. His mother had to get a job and move into the cheapest apartment she could find in what he always says was the worst all-black neighborhood in the city. Her boyfriend at the time, my father's father, moved in with her to help support her and her new baby, but he left them both after just a few months. Dad never grew up with a father, so it's no surprise that he doesn't know how to interact with his kids. He works nights at a factory downtown, so Shawn and I only see him before leaving for school as he's getting home. Our interaction is usually a couple of words, and then we part ways. I barely know who the guy is. In our handful of interactions, he's always been a very stern man, quick to talk about how "hard his life has been" and how I "just need to find the courage and deal with life."

How could I possibly bring up that I'm getting bullied? I can hear him now, "*You*?! Bullied? Parker's men don't get bullied," he'd scoff at me while straightening his collar, "The only people who get bullied are weak, and I know I didn't raise you weak. You better man up and keep focused. Why are you even worried about what others think of you? You know you should be worrying about your grades. Scholarships don't go to kids who are worried about *bullies*."

I know my dad means well, but God, I can't stand him sometimes. All I've ever really wanted was an ounce of sympathy from the guy. I know he might never be proud of me. After all, what I want to do will never be something he approves of, but if he could act for one minute like I'm his son and not just be disappointed, I'd thank God for finally listening. He and my mother both have little faith in me. They laugh when I talk about becoming a famous artist or having an exhibit in a museum one day. It's like I'm one big joke to them.

Maybe it's true, or perhaps I am a joke.

"Mr. Parker? Mr. Parker!" Suddenly my eyes snapped forward and out of the dream state that I was trapped inside.

"Yes?" I sighed out, making sheepish eye contact with my English teacher looming over me, clearly having caught me not paying attention.

"Could you please tell me, Mr. Parker, what Shakespeare might have meant to signify with the blood on Lady Macbeth's hands?" the teacher asked with a grin as if to embarrass me in front of the whole class for zoning out, not hanging on his every last pretentious word.

"Her irreconcilable guilt. That's why she can't seem to get it off her hands no matter how hard she tries." I started back, watching him swallow back the condescending speech he was ready to present. I already finished the whole book last week; I love reading. I don't love my English teacher or his need to try to make me look bad.

"Right, Drew." The teacher stammered, shifting his gaze to another victim, "Bryan, could you tell me why that is significant to Lady Macbeth's character?" Bryan, another son-of-a-

Karen on the football team dressed as an outlet mall mannequin, looked back from his conversation with some blonde girl wrapped around his finger.

"Uh, is it because she killed Juliet?" The teacher looked confused,

"No, Bryan, Juliet is from another Shakespeare play. I suspect you have a couple of pages in your 'Shakespeare for Dummies' book glued together. Stay after class, won't you?"

Bryan scoffed, "Whatever. I don't have time to read this. Figures that Drew knows the answer, he's too fat to do anything else but read old English guys make up pretend stories about men in tights." The whole class erupted in laughter.

"Damn, Bryan, I would assume you, a white man who is always wearing those tight football pants, would know ALL about every other white, privileged man in tights that we read about in this class! "All I could do was look down at my book in embarrassment, I wish I could tell him off like I wanted to, but I'm not about to get into another fight this year.

"Settle down, boys. That's enough.", our teacher barks, surprised at my clap back.

My next class went on uneventfully, which sounds boring, but to me, it is a sigh of relief.

Anytime I can get through a class without having my body, my pizza face, my differences called to attention, I will take it as a significant victory. I get so few in my life that I have to get them where I can. When the bell rang for lunch, I trudged to my locker, loading my books in as slowly as possible to kill as much time as I could before I'd have to enter the throne room for the high school elite where I was nothing but a court jester there for their entertainment. Finally, I headed to my usual table for one, no reservations needed to eat whatever lunchroom delicacy they were serving up. Was it chicken and macaroni day or macaroni and chicken day? Who could recall? About halfway through my meal, as I was just starting to think maybe I'd get a break today, I looked up to see two of the football players playing catch with another kid's pudding cup.

"Poor kid, but at least it's not me," I thought to myself, when suddenly one of them chucked the dessert in my direction, hitting me square in the head, exploding all over me on impact. "Oh hell no!" I shouted, immediately wiping it from my face.

"You know, it does kind of look like crap, doesn't it?" chuckled out the one jock with tears in his eyes from laughter. "Dude! They say you are what you eat, so enjoy the treat "Pudding Cup" the other boy said between chuckles winking at me and blowing me a kiss before high fiving his friend and sitting back down at their table. All I could hear before running to the bathroom were giggles, whispers, and not-so-subtle insults. I shoved open the doors to the hall and booked it to the bathroom, trying to minimize the number of witnesses to what was already a hall of fame embarrassing moment.

I barreled into the bathroom door shoulder first, leaving pudding behind on every surface I touched. I looked at myself in the mirror to see streaks of tears wiping away the offending chocolate substance from my face. Silently, I grabbed fistfuls of paper towels and ran into the first stall. No matter how hard I tried, I couldn't stop the tears from flooding out while I wiped as much pudding off me as I could see.

My mind started racing, "Get it together, Drew. What's the matter with you? God, you're such a loser". It was like all the hurt I had felt till now was rising to the surface.

Abruptly I heard the bathroom door slam open, "I still can't believe you hit him *perfectly* in his ugly head, man! Coach better take you off the bench this weekend with that arm." One football player's voice praised, clearly ecstatic about the trauma they caused.

"Yeah, dude, I can still see his face now as that pudding exploded like a bomb all over him. 'Who me? Why can't you just leave me alone?'" the other jock responded, mimicking my voice to sound like a little girl's. I quickly put my hand over my mouth and pulled my feet up off the floor to hopefully avoid being seen.

"You know, sometimes I do feel kind of bad for the guy, but he makes it so easy to mess with him. Why not push his head around like a pinball. My dad has always said, "If niggers aren't good at sports, then they have no purpose in this country. I think he's pretty spot on with that one." The two laughed more and casually strolled out of the room, letting the door slam behind them, piercing through the sudden silence of the space. However, it was almost deafening with the thoughts racing in my head. Why are they so concerned about the color of my skin? Of course, they think I'm a loser; everyone does. I wish sometimes they'd think so little of me they'd pretend I was invisible instead of putting a target on my back for just being black. Maybe I should find a way to get back at them. Sure, I might get in a fight and possibly be expelled. I don't care anymore. Anything is better than living in this hell every single day. I had to find a way to intimidate the guys on the team. Maybe if they were afraid of me retaliating, then they wouldn't mess with me anymore. I could sneak into the locker room and mess with all of their gear or spray paint something on their cars in the parking lot during lunch. I have to get them back somehow. I can't just sit back and take it anymore.

I forced myself to wipe away my tears, blow my nose and get to my locker to cover up my stained shirt with my hoodie before Spanish. Oh no, Spanish class. I didn't even think of the fact I'd have to face my torturers just an hour after they humiliated me in front of the whole school. "Just get through this, and you'll be free, Drew." I thought to myself. "After this, you have art class with your favorite teacher, and you can keep working on your drawing; you love drawing. Just focus. It's just six, ten-minute segments you have to get through. You can make it through almost anything for ten minutes." Repeating "Just ten minutes." over and over to myself mentally as I walked to Spanish class. I took a huge breath in as I walked through the door frame and directly to my desk keeping my eyes trained on the floor. Quickly I sat down and picked up my Spanish textbook, pretending to read to avoid everyone while mostly just wishing the floor would open up and swallow me whole. I hear my tormentors burst into the classroom, laughing, joking, and moving with unmatched confidence. When will the white privilege in this school stop?

Without looking up from my book, I could feel their eyes on me. The bell rang to signal class was in session, and so began my internal stopwatch, counting down each ten-minute increment second by second. "Nine minutes, fifty-nine seconds, nine minutes, fifty-eight seconds, nine minutes, fifty-seven seconds." I could do this. Spanish seemed as standard as usual, or maybe I'm so preoccupied with surviving that it makes everything pale in comparison. "six minutes, thirty-eight seconds, six minutes, thirty-seven seconds." I barely can concentrate on any questions, conjugating verbs, or even on the ungodly shriek of my Spanish teacher's voice. Her octave could have shattered windows had there been any in this prison of a school. Spanish has always been one of the classes where I feel the most insecure. You'd think being half Mexican, Spanish would come naturally to me, but you'd be wrong.

"Four minutes, forty-two seconds, four minutes, forty-one seconds." My grandparents immigrating to America squelched their cultural roots to assimilate into their new surroundings as seamlessly as possible. They learned English as quickly as possible. They stopped speaking Spanish in front of their kids, stopped cooking Mexican food, celebrating Mexican holidays, listening to Spanish music, everything. Anything tying them to their past ceased to exist, and so, to my mom, it felt like a secret she must hide to further herself in this country. "Two minutes, thirty-one seconds, two minutes, twenty-nine seconds." To my brother and me, these traditions were nonexistent. When class schedules came out at the beginning of the semester, my mom strongly encouraged (forced) me to take French classes rather than Spanish. I had to beg her to let me switch because it interfered with me getting to

do art class, the only reason I can force myself
to go to school most days. She agreed after days
of pleading, and after pointing out, I could
always take French next year.

Chapter 4: Perfect Planning

I sit across from my mother at the dinner table. She sits with a stone-cold look in her eyes. Nothing ever gets under her skin anymore. She and my father are emotionless shells of the people they used to be, and it has turned out to be such a disservice to their children. How am I supposed to talk to them and tell them what's happening to me? Should I even bother? I know without skipping a beat exactly what their reactions will be. My mother will turn to me and say, "Drew, I don't want to hear about this. It would be best if you handled this on your own. I got much worse as a child, and I turned out fine."

"Yeah. Thanks, mom." What else was there for me to say. Her reactions sting my ears now. They were constantly dripping in apathy, wrapped in the monotonous tone of her voice.

Compared to my father, her reaction is a warm ray of sunshine on my skin. The man doesn't even pretend to give a damn, and if I told him that someone at school was bullying me, he'd probably laugh in my face. He had a different experience than me as a child, I understand that, but some sympathy wouldn't kill these people, would it? My dad had to deal with growing up in the inner city. I'm sure bullies were the least of his worries. From the stories he's told me, it was more about surviving the night when he was left alone in a run-down, barely secure apartment in the projects. I get that our struggles are different, and I'm sympathetic to what he went through. I just wish he could return the favor.

Shawn sits next to me, quiet, awkwardly shoveling mashed potatoes into his mouth. He, better than the rest of the family, understands what's happening to me. After all, Shawn is the one that suggested that I tell somebody. Some part of me believes that he knows it'll fall on deaf ears, but I appreciate his attempt to help me relieve some of the pain and anxiety this is causing. Shawn's experiences differ from mine now, though. In middle school, sure, Shawn understood some of what was happening to me. We were both the only black kids in our school, and Shawn, being a year older, started to get bullied by some of his older classmates. He never spoke about it to mom and dad, but one morning, right as we stepped off the bus, one of his classmates ran up to the door of the bus and tripped Shawn as he was stepping down onto the sidewalk. The entire crowd in front of the school erupted in laughter as though they were in on the plan. I don't know if it was just the innocence of being a year younger, not mature enough to be so cruel to each other, but I didn't understand why someone would do that. At that moment, I didn't know what to do. I tried to help Shawn onto his feet, but he turned to me, looking more embarrassed than I'd seen him ever before. "Leave me alone!" he yelled in my face and ran off, disappearing into the crowd of kids.

It wasn't long after that that Shawn started to act out in anger. The slightest inconvenience would set him off. He began to get into fights at school and home. I could hear his voice bellowing from inside his room, trying to start a war with our parents about any little thing. I distinctly remember that our parents showed little concern, calling it a "phase." Shawn's saving grace was the summer that our father made him try out for the football team.

"It'll be good for you, kid. Get some of that anger out.", he said. I can only imagine that our father was the same as a child. He happened to stumble onto the football team with coaxing from no one around him, but it gave him a way to channel his anger and trauma. See, our father only knows how to parent through experience, and luckily for Shawn, their experiences were more similar.

I'm not similar to any of the people sitting around this table.

We finished our dinner in silence, apart from the chewing noises and utensils clanging against the plates.

Shawn and I ritualistically wash the dishes and clean the table. We had been trained from a young age to always clean up after a meal.

"Hey, have you told them about what's going on with the guys giving you shit at school yet?" Shawn asked.

"No. It wouldn't do any good. Mom and Dad will just ignore me."

"You don't know that, Drew. It would at least be good for you to try, and if they blow you off, then go to the principal or something?"

"You mean the guy that's itching at the chance to kick me out of school?" I asked. "I'm sure that'll go over well. He'd probably jump right in to fight them for me." Shawn's eyes dropped. He knew I was right. "Look, I'll try to talk to mom, but there's no way I'm talking to dad about any of this. I don't want any more lectures from the guy."

"Do you want me to talk to him, Drew?"

"Why, so you guys can laugh about it together? No, thank you." I knew instantly I shouldn't have said it that way. "Sorry. I didn't mean to say that." I muttered before he got the chance to respond.

"No, it's cool. I understand. Let me know what mom says." Shawn finished drying the last plate and turned to walk off to his room. "Don't put it off. Talk to her.", he said.

I nodded my head in agreement and watched Shawn walk out of the kitchen and down the hall. The thud of his door shutting behind him echoed in my ears for the next few minutes. I knew I had to talk to my mom, to someone, or things had no chance of getting any better. That thought didn't make it any easier of a task to complete, though.

As if by some divine cosmic intervention, my mom walked into the kitchen seconds after Shawn left, and in her broken English, asked, "Are you guys done cleaning up?".

"Yeah, mom, we are." I hadn't worked up the courage to say anything, but I knew she wouldn't bring up my feelings on her own. Finally, this was it, the moment I had to take, like it or not. I opened my mouth and tried to spit out the words, "Mom, can we talk?".

"Sure," she said. "What is it?"

"Listen, I know you probably don't care, but I have to talk to somebody about what's happening to me at school."

"What is it, Drew? What's happening?"

"There are these guys from the football team, and they're making my life a living hell!"

"Language!" she asserted. I was surprised that *that* is what concerned her.

I already knew the direction this conversation was going. "Mom, they're going to push me to get into a fight again, and you know what the school said last time. I don't want to get kicked out of school for defending myself."

"Drew—" I had to cut her off. I knew what she was going to say, but she just doesn't get it.

"They're the reason I came home the other day with my clothes stained. They threw food at me at lunch. I didn't fall into the mud on my walk home. They torture me EVERY DAY. I can't take it anymore. I don't know what to do. I hate going to school. I HATE IT!" By this point, I was hysterical. I felt the tears on my cheeks running down to my chin. I don't usually cry in front of my family. There's just no point to it, but I couldn't hold this in any longer. The weeks and weeks of torture had all built up. Whenever someone called me fat, or stupid, or whatever it was, I held it in. I couldn't contain it anymore.

"Drew, get ahold of yourself. It can't be that bad." Of course, she thinks it isn't that bad. Why would she believe me? "I think we should talk to your father about this."

"No, mom. He'll just make fun of me and tell me to suck it up."

"Maybe so, but that might be what you need to hear, Drew." She cannot be serious.

"Honestly, just forget I said anything. I'll just deal with it." I walked out of the kitchen before I could see the look of disappointment on her face. I knew she wouldn't take me seriously. There isn't a point in talking to them about it, and Shawn isn't much help either. I guess I'm in this alone. I walked down the hall to my room and shut the door behind me. I can't win trying to convince my family that I'm struggling with this. Nobody is taking me seriously with this.

Waking up the following day, knowing that nobody was on my side, was near impossible, but I did it. I woke up and made a plan. There's no way I was showing my face in school today. I heard Shawn's door creak open, his footsteps sneak into the bathroom, and the shower turned on. It was finally my chance to escape without anyone knowing. I ran to the bathroom door and yelled out, "Hey Shawn, I'm walking today. I'll see you at school." I didn't wait for an answer before grabbing my bag and running out the front door.

I just want to be alone today. There's an old, rusted-out metal bridge in the woods behind our neighborhood.

I found it one day after a fight with my dad. I left the house in a hurry and didn't know where to go, so I just started wondering. I eventually stumbled onto this old gray bridge with train tracks running over it. From that moment on, it's where I go when I just need to think. The path is at the fence line of our house. It sits at the back of the subdivision, near the tree line. It's just about a mile walk, and at the end of the path, it opens into a clearing large enough for the bridge. There's a creek running underneath the bridge. It's small, but the sound of the water is cathartic.

I leave through the front door, sneaking around the side of the house and around the back fence to get to the path before Shawn can get out of the shower and catch me red-handed. The trail looks grown over since the last time I walked it a couple of months ago. I know the path like the back of my hand, so stepping over a few fallen branches isn't an issue. I set my anxiety-ridden brain to autopilot and keep one foot in front of the other as I begin to dissect my situation. I can't go on like this anymore. Jake and the other guys at school are tormenting me for fun. Shawn isn't able to do anything to help because his ego is too big, and my parents won't listen to me for shit. I feel more alone right now than I have ever felt before. Nobody understands me, nobody listens, and it seems like nobody cares lately. I'm stuck in this world alone, not knowing if it ever gets any better.

My eyes flicker as if to get my mind's attention. The wooded path has opened up, and before me sits a pitch-black room. I swiftly turn to my left, then my right, and behind me. There is nothing but black. Am I dreaming? Am I hallucinating? "Hello?" I call out, but there is no answer. The room is so dark around me, swallowing me whole, and I feel an intense sadness wash over me. The loneliness I'm feeling is in its physical form. I cannot see or hear anyone around me. The most actual and utterly lonely feeling seeps into my bones, and I can't move. "Hello? Anyone?" I scream louder, all while being swallowed by the black hole that is this room. I feel a crunch beneath my left foot, and the lonely room glitches, revealing the same path I was on. The sun, so bright, stings both of my eyes. What was that? I must've been completely out of it to imagine something like that, but that feeling of physical loneliness was so familiar.

The fog clears from my mind, and I can see, despite the blinding sun, that I'm already at the bridge.

The weeds around the creek have grown higher than my chest, but the path to the tracks is still intact. It's a steep hill up to the railroad tracks, but I can make it on all fours. The trail still has few stones I can use to get a foothold and push myself up. I make my way up, drop my bag on the track and take my customary seat on the ledge of the bridge. My feet hang down over the creek. This bridge is the only place I've felt at peace, not worried about what will happen to me next or what anyone is thinking about the way I dress, nothing. Just a place that I can take a deep breath and let go of the anxiety that plagues my mind every single day. This place is magical.

Sitting on the bridge above the running water, I can't help but think about what has been going on. What am I going to do if nobody will listen to what I'm saying? I'm struggling, and I feel so alone in what I'm going through. I tried to talk to my mom, but she blew me off as she usually does. What do I do next?

Maybe if the guys at school are scared of me, they won't mess with me so much. If I can't fight them, then I'll have to think of something else. Think, Drew. Come on!

A prank. That's it!

That's what I have to do. If I mess with the bullies, maybe they'll stop. I can't pull the pudding trick or anything at lunch, for that matter. They'll see it coming. Perhaps if they don't know I did it, they'll stop messing with everyone in the school altogether. I need to do something when none of them are around, but what?

Wait, they're all on the football team. Maybe I can do something while the team is in practice or after all the guys leave for the day! I usually stay after school in Pierce's class anyway. I'll be there the whole time. What if I snuck into the locker room after class? They usually lock up when they leave, but I bet I could convince Shawn to "forget" to lock up. I could sneak into the locker room and cover their gear in paint. They wouldn't even see it until the next day! This plan is genius, and I know they won't suspect a thing. The only downside is that if they did somehow find out that it was me, they'd no doubt try to start a fight, but this school is gunning for me to get expelled anyway. I might as well go out with a bang. Who cares, right?

Well, that's the plan then. Maybe someone getting back at these guys will give them a taste of how it feels to be the victim of bullying. Best case scenario, they never find out who messed with their gear, and they finally leave me alone. Worst case, I don't have to go back to school. Win-Win.

I spent the rest of that day out on that bridge, taking in what could be the last peaceful feeling I'd feel. If my plan worked, I'd be in the clear, but if not, things might be completely different. Either way, I wasn't backing out. I made my plan, and I was going to stick to it. Shawn could help me if he wanted to, or he could back out and keep his ego protected. I was finally at the point where none of it mattered. It was my chance to get my revenge, and there was nothing that would stop me. It was almost sunset before I started my walk back home. Shawn knew I wasn't at school, and I'm sure they tried to call mom. Luckily, she's never able to answer at work and doesn't check the machine's messages at home. Shawn won't rat me out, and I know that. I'll need to talk to him when I get home to get his help with the plan. I know he's been looking for a way to help me out, and this is it.

I slid down the dirt hill from the tracks, covering the back of my pants in the dirt, and made my way back to the path. I headed home with a new feeling of confidence that couldn't break again. I'd get to school tomorrow, act as if everything is normal, then after practice; I'd sneak into the locker room and get the payback I've always wanted. I can't wait to see the look on their faces when they see all of their gear destroyed.

On the other side of the path behind the house, popping back through, and the sun has almost set. I know I'm about to run into an onslaught of questions from Shawn about where I've been today. I follow the fence line, and when I get to the front of the house, I notice something out of place. Dad's truck is in the driveway. He's never here around this time. He's usually just getting to work to start his overnight shift. Something was going on. Part of me wasn't wanting to go home. Something in me told me to run back to the bridge and just spend the rest of the night there, but I didn't have the chance. I started to turn around and heard the handle of the door begin to turn.

The front door flung open, and Shawn poked his head out. "Dude, where have you been all day? Everyone is home, and they want to talk to us. I don't know what's going on."

"I was taking some time for myself today. I'll be there in a sec." I should've started to run while I could.

"Hurry." Shawn sounded more demanding than usual.

I hustled to my room to throw down my bag and change, and by the time I walked back into the living room, everyone was sitting down, just waiting for me. I can't help but wonder if mom said anything about the bullies. Dad isn't the type to skip work for something like that. Maybe it's something more significant. I treaded lightly into the living room, walked past my mom, and took my seat on the couch next to Shawn.

Dad had a beer in his hand. He didn't normally drink, at least not usually in front of us. "Listen, guys," he sighed a painful sigh, "I've gotten laid off from my job at the factory. The plant had been talking about layoffs for a while now. I thought that I wouldn't be affected, but it turns out that they're cutting most of the guys that have been there for years."

"Dad, what does that mean? What are we going to do?" Shawn was becoming more agitated with every word.

"Your mom is still working, but our income isn't going to be what it used to. The plant isn't offering any severance for me, and we have no savings."

"Do we need to get jobs to help?" I asked, feeling like I had to chip in with an idea.

Mom did the same. "Anything is an option at this point, guys. My income won't support all of us, but we're looking at a few different options that we need to talk about."

"We're going to be moving either way. We can't afford rent in this neighborhood anymore, even if I get a job paying the same. We've been struggling to keep up as it is." Dad seemed flustered. "We're going to have to move in with your grandmother in the city. She has a couple of extra rooms for us, but it's just until we can get on our feet. We'll likely have to stay in the city, maybe an apartment. It's all we'll be able to afford.

"But what about school? My friends?" Shawn *would* be concerned about his friends.

"I'm good. Can I go pack now?" I asked, eyeing Shawn.

"We have the rest of this month, but we have to be out by the 30th. We've already talked to the landlord about leaving. Guys, we're going to have to get rid of a lot, there's no room in mom's house, and if we do get an apartment, there may be even less room there. You'll both be at a new school, but we'll figure that out when we get settled." Mom had a deflated look in her eyes.

Shawn snapped, yelling, "This is bullshit. It's not fair!"

"Shawn! It isn't your decision. I don't care what's fair and what's not." Our father's voice boomed across the room, and it shut Shawn down immediately. He stood up and walked to his room, his head sinking lower and lower with each step.

"Drew, are you good?" Dad switched his focus to me.

"Yeah. I'm fine. I'm ready to go." I have no friends to leave behind as Shawn does. They know that, for me, this could be a blessing more than anything. It makes my plan to mess with the football team even more effortless. I can't get expelled if I'm already leaving. This move is coming at the perfect time for me. I know Shawn is going to hate it, though. He's gotten used to being the popular one around school, and now he'll have to start over. "Shawn's going to be pissed, though. He has it easy at school. He's friends with everyone." I said.

"He's just going to have to get over it." There's the father I've come to know. Not concerned about how his son feels. I almost thought he was starting to care for a second. I'm glad we're back to normal.

"Fine by me. I'm going to start packing if that's cool." I stood up. They seemed shocked at how well I was taking everything, but they must not recognize that I have nothing to lose here. This place has become nothing but stress and disappointment for me.

I wanted to start packing immediately, but I knew I still needed to talk to Shawn. Now that nothing was stopping me from getting one last hit in with the football guys, I was ready to execute my plan more than ever. I needed his help, though. Using the knuckles of my first two fingers, I tapped on his door. I waited a minute for an answer, but there was nothing.

"Shawn?" I knocked again.

"What?" He sounded flat, not normal.

"Can I come in?"

"Uh-yeah. Sure."

I turned the knob to his bedroom door and let it swing open. Standing in the doorway, I could see him face down on his bed, loathing the thought of what was to come. I know he's not used to being checked in on or having anyone concerned about his emotional state, and I know how that feels. The least I could do was be the one person in this family with the emotional capacity to check on someone's well-being.

"How do you feel about what just happened?" I asked. He raised his head, showing off a puzzled look painted all over his face.

"Why do you care? I'm sure you're happy to get out of that school."

"I'm not mad about it, but I asked how you felt. I know you have a different experience there, and I'm sure you do not want to leave." I said, knowing that was already the truth.

"I hate that you have it so rough there, I do, but I genuinely like going to school and having everyone know my name. I understand that you don't like the rest of the guys on the team because they mess with you so much, but it's different for me, Drew. I can't help it." I can see Shawn starting to tear up.

"I get it, dude. I'd never want to leave if I were in your shoes. Trust me, I wish I were, but no matter what school we go to, you'll be the one that fits in. Just join another team, and you'll be in the same position. Maybe your teammates won't try to punch me every day there." I wasn't trying to make him feel bad, but I could see it in his face that he did.

"I'm sorry, Drew. I shouldn't be letting shit like that happen to you, but you know it's hard for me to do anything. Jake and the other guys are just a step away from targeting me if I try to do anything."

"Shawn, I get it. You don't want to risk being like me—"

Before I could finish my thought, Shawn interrupted. "It's not like that, and you know that."

"No, it is like that, but it's ok. I understand what you're going through. There is something you could do to help me, though." That puzzled look fell over him again. "I want to get a little payback before we leave. Nothing major. Just some sort of goodbye present, just to mess with the team a little bit." He was sitting up at this point, stunned that I would have the gall to plan something to get back at the team.

"Honestly, dude, I owe you at least that. I've been acting like a jerk this school year. I should've just said to hell with my reputation and stood up for you when they were treating you like a punching bag. I'm sorry that I wasn't there for you." He was surprisingly endearing. I'd never had him apologize to me for anything before.

"It's all good. I just need your help tomorrow after school. I want to sneak into the locker room after practice is over. I see you guys locking up after from the art room a few doors down. I want you to stay behind, wait until they're all gone, and leave the locker room door unlocked for me."

"W-what are you going to do in there?" He seemed on board but stunned that he would even try anything like this.

"Pierce always leaves the art supply cabinet open for me since I stay after school, waiting for you. I'm just going to take some paint and leave the team a 'goodbye note' or something like that."

"What do you mean by a goodbye note?" Shawn cracked a smile. He couldn't resist a good prank.

"Shawn, don't worry about it. It's on me. Just leave the door unlocked tomorrow after practice and wait for me outside by the side door, ok?"

"Alright, man, just don't get caught. You're lucky I owe you one."

Everything was in place now. This prank was going to be incredible. I turned around with a smile on my face and left Shawn to start packing. For the first time that I can remember, I was excited to get to school tomorrow.

Time flew by that day. Maybe it was the anticipation; perhaps it was sheer adrenaline. I was ready to finally get my revenge on the guys that had been making my life hell at school. I only had two weeks left here anyway. They wouldn't have time to retaliate, and if they did, it wouldn't matter anyway. By the time my last class rolled around, I was shaking so bad that I couldn't draw. Pierce must've known something was going on because he kept stopping by my desk to check on me.

"Not making much progress there, D. Are you doing alright?"

"Yeah, just taking some time to think. I'm good." I said, trying not to smile.

The bell rang at the end of the day. I stayed behind in the art room like every other day. Pierce sat down next to me after everyone was out of the room for the day.

"You sure you're alright, D?" he asked.

"I'm good. Just a lot going on, I guess." Pierce was probably the only thing I'd miss about this school. He was the only teacher that stood up for me. "My family is moving at the end of the month. I'm going to have to move to another school, I guess."

He looked at me with what I can only assume was sadness. "That's a shame, D. You're a good student and a good kid."

"Thanks, Pierce. You're no doubt the best teacher here. I'll miss you for sure."

"Do me a favor, D. When you get to that next school, stay out of trouble. You're a good guy. Don't worry about what anyone else says. Just be you." His advice always seemed so easy to follow on paper, but there's so much more to follow in real life.

"Will do," I said with a smile.

Pierce jogged back to his desk to grab his things before leaving. "You know the drill. Lock up when you leave, ok?"

"Yeah, no problem. Thanks, Pierce." He looked at me with a grin and winked, then was off. The door slammed behind him. The slam of the door echoed in my head for what seemed like the next twenty minutes. The plan was getting closer and closer, and I was so nervous that I was shaking.

The supply cabinet was in the opposite corner of my desk. It was a deep blue, rickety metal cabinet about a foot taller than me. The cabinet was full to the brim with every color of paint you could imagine-Acrylics, oils, and spray paint. It had everything. Seven shelves were full of everything I would ever need to get back at these guys. I grabbed the first can of spray paint I found, 'Midnight Black.' It seems fitting since that's the only color that bothers these guys.

The art room's door had a small rectangular window on the left side of the door, positioned just perfectly enough to see the entrance to the back of the locker rooms. I had to wait long enough to see Shawn leave. He should be the last one out if he does everything the way I asked him to. The locker room door bounces open, and a few of the players come out into the hallway, Jake being one of them. I had to stop myself from busting through the door and cracking his head open with this paint can. After a few minutes, most of the team had left through the school's side door, but I still hadn't seen Shawn. There's no way he'd bail on me.

Just as my concern that Shawn wouldn't pull through was at an all-time high, I saw the door swing open one last time. His round face creeped out from behind it, and I felt a wave of relief wash over my entire body. He looked around for a couple of minutes before catching my gaze through the small window of the art room door. He flashed a thumbs up and turned to walk down the hall and out the exit door. It was finally my chance to get back at these guys for what seemed like a lifetime of torture.

I took my chance, busting through the art room door as if I were a Bond villain, breaking into a bank vault to steal the world's most valuable blood diamond. I'd tumble past the guards shooting each one between the eyes, drop to the floor, and cut off the thumb of one guard to obtain fingerprint access into the vault. I'd maneuver through the laser-equipped alarm system with ease, snatch the diamond from its case, and be gone before anyone knew I was there.

Back to reality, I shuffled across the hallway between the two rooms, opened the locker room door, and entered, making sure nobody saw me from either side. The locker room is like a figure eight of bright red lockers with a concrete floor and mirrors along both sides. I'm able to use the mirrors to my advantage, looking around corners to ensure nobody is there to watch me.

The football team had a row of lockers along the back wall. I knew this from seeing the gear in there in P.E. last semester. The players had always had those lockers. It was a tradition at this school. A good luck charm, maybe. Most of the guys who used the locker room had a

70

padlock, but most football teams didn't. I think their egos were big enough to trust that nobody would mess with their stuff. Nobody ever dared to challenge any of the football team guys for fear of having their skulls crushed in on the gym floor.

I knew Shawn's locker was seventy-three, the same as the number on his jersey, but I pulled the gear out of every other locker in the row. Seventy-one? Check. Seventy-five? Check. By the time I finished, there were helmets, shoulder pads, and red and white jerseys all over the locker room floor. The paint rattled as I shook it, preparing to ruin every jersey there. I popped the cap off and began spraying. The black color muddied up every jersey on the floor until you could no longer see any of the numbers. I flipped them all and committed the same atrocity on the opposite side. I couldn't stop myself from laughing the entire time. "This will teach those privileged assholes!" I left a little red and white fabric showing; Just enough so the team could tell what happened. I slammed every locker in the row shut and turned my back to leave. Just as I was about to make my exit to safety, I thought of another genius plan. My back turned to the door, and I popped the lid off of the spray can once more. It rattled a little louder. The paint was almost gone, but I had enough for one last message.

Spray.

Swipe.

Spray.

Swipe.

The bold black letters on the front of the lockers spelled out 'C-R-A-C-K-E-R-S.' There's no hiding who would be responsible for writing it. Still, I had absolutely nothing to lose in this game anymore, and if they were going to target me for the color of my skin, I was going to send it back to them tenfold. More pleased with my actions than I had ever been before, I turned to exit. Looking back at the disaster I created once more, and I laughed out loud this time. Even I'm surprised I had the guts to do that; I know I'll pay for it later. I feel so victorious right now. The door creaked open, and I pushed the lock on the handle to ensure I locked it tight behind me. There was a new skip in my step as I walked to the art room to put the spray can back, grab my bag, and lock it up. Tomorrow would be a fun day, that's for sure.

I have never slept as sound as I did last night. I got home feeling so accomplished, so confident, and I woke up this morning with energy as I've never had before. I can't wait to see the look on the team's faces when they see what happened. Maybe it'll knock them down a few rungs. God, I'm so ready for that.

I wanted to avoid any conversation with Shawn, fearing he would judge me for what happened, so I decided to get to school on foot today. I set out the front door with newfound confidence. My feet, pounding the pavement to the music, stepped one in front of the other without pause. I felt invincible today. The couple-mile walk wouldn't phase me.

I stepped into the crystal-clear front doors of my high school, sauntered over to the vending machine for my ritual morning Dr. Pepper, and got a head start to Pierce's Room to drop off my sketchbooks. The stairs to the lower level were bursting at the seams, and there were people already gathered around the locker room door. I pushed my way through the freshman that had no doubt never seen anything like this, down the stairs and to the art room entrance. Time moved at half the speed as I crossed the hallway, eyes transfixed on the commotion near the locker room. A few of the cheerleaders were outside the doors, crying.

"So dramatic," I thought to myself. The cheerleaders always took turns laughing at the racist comments thrown my way. God forbid they experience any hate. Time sped up instantly; I rolled my eyes and headed in to see Mr. Pierce.

"What's going on out there?" I said innocently, trying not to smirk.

"Oh, you don't know? Someone vandalized some of the lockers in there. I haven't seen anything, but it makes you wonder who could've had access to that room when nobody was around." Was he insinuating that I could've done it? Is he on to me?

"Yeah, weird," I said, dismissing his claim. "Well, I have to get to class. See you in a few hours."

My first-hour class approached with a more unsettling feeling. I hope Pierce doesn't figure anything out and rat me out to the principal or anything. At least I had Macbeth to distract me in this class. I was relieved for a split second, but the more we read, the more I remembered the underlying theme of 'the conscience coming back to haunt someone.' The themes of guilt and betrayal started to seep into my brain. Was what I did wrong of me to do, despite all the hate that had come my way? I have to stop thinking about it, or my brain is going to explode. I reach down to my bag, pull out my sketchbook and start drawing my anxiety away.

The next hour went by in proper anti-climactic form and then lunch. Lunch was more abnormal than usual. Everyone was whispering, pointing fingers, and on the verge of rioting. I think everyone in the school had heard what happened to the team and collectively tried to solve the mystery. It felt awkwardly similar to the board game Clue. I knew I was the killer, but nobody else had any idea. They were all collectively a few steps away from putting the puzzle pieces together. It was Drew, in the locker room, with the spray can. Bam! They caught me.

I took my place in the line for hot lunch, grabbed my tray, and kept my eyes on the unruly crowd in the lunchroom. Who knew? Which pair of eyes would meet mine and solve the riddle? I got through the line successfully with what looked like slop on my lunch tray. I guess that was a waste. I'll have to make a trip to the vending machine after this. I put my tray down at the first empty table I could find, but when I looked up, I saw Shawn's eyes piercing through the crowd and into mine. He was disappointed, worried, upset. I couldn't pinpoint what he was feeling, but I knew it wasn't good. He flicked his head toward the row of vending machines as if to usher me that way with just a motion of his head. I knew he was pissed, so I obeyed. We met at the furthest machine from the crowd.

"Drew, what the hell, man?" He whispered but screamed at the same time.
"What?"

"You didn't tell me you were going to vandalize everything in there. Why would you do that?"

"You know what they put me through. That's the very least I could do. Those guys deserve it."

"Yeah, maybe so, but you didn't even touch my locker. Do you know how suspicious that looks to everyone? I've already had some of the players ask if I did anything. You know they're going to catch on to you sooner or later!" He had a good point.

"I didn't want to mess up your things. I didn't think anyone would notice. Who cares, though, Shawn. We're leaving this school in a couple of weeks. Nobody is going to find out by then, and if they do, so what? Do they expel me? I'm leaving anyway."

I felt a presence behind me, and Shawn's eyes widened just before his head dropped. "Shit." I thought, "this is it." I knew it was Jake before I even turned around.

"Hey, tough guy!" Jake had a knack for coming up with shitty nicknames. "Word around here is that you're the one who messed with our stuff.

"Jake, leave him alone. He didn't do anything." Shawn finally defended me.

Jake barked back, "Stay out of it, Shawn."

"You know what, Jake, yeah. I did it, and I don't care. I ruined all of your shit, but it's nothing compared to the hell you and your "boys" have been putting me through. What did I ever do to you guys, huh?" I was letting it all out, loud enough for the whole lunchroom to hear.

"See you guys. I told you it was this nigger!"

My vision turned red. Blood dripped down over my eyes, and I saw nothing but hatred. The blood in my veins boiled and overflowed. That was the final straw. The last time I would stand for it. The last time I would hold myself back.

I cocked my fist back and lunged at Jake with every ounce of strength I had ever had, making contact with his right temple. Jake hit the floor, and I didn't hesitate for a second before jumping on top of him. I drove a knee into his stomach and a fist into his throat. I must've gotten in three, maybe four good hits, before Shawn grabbed me from behind, trying to stop me. I turned and pushed Shawn back a few feet, but I saw two of the other players running full speed at me with a chair when I turned around. I raised my hands to cover my face before dropping to my knees, but it was too late. I felt a stabbing pain above my eye, and the red turned swiftly to black.

Chapter 5: Greener Grass?

Clothes and books are all over my room in no particular fashion. It looks like a comic book war zone. I've spent my days trying to decide what to keep, what to donate, and what to throw away. Tomorrow is the day we move to the city. Mom and Dad found a cheap enough apartment, so we don't have to move in with grandma. I'm sure Dad would've hated that. He doesn't exactly get along with his mother-in-law, but they're at least able to be civil in passing. I'm glad that we're going to have a place of our own to live in, even if Shawn and I have to share a room for a bit, at least until we can afford a bigger house.

The piles of comic books are organized alphabetically and numerically by issue. I have to cut the bundles down to just two and sell the rest. The bedrooms are small, and whatever we can't sell, we have to donate. I haven't been to school in the last two weeks, not since the fight. The faculty found out that I had admitted to spray-painting the locker rooms. They threatened to press charges, but since some of the players ganged up on me, they dropped them and decided that expulsion was punishment enough. I only have a black eye and a few cuts on my lip and cheek. I heard Jake went to the hospital. His parents tried to press charges, but when they found out everything Jake had put me through this last year, plus the fact that he was the instigator of the fight, they pretty much gave up on that. Dad came home last night and told us that he had a second interview for some warehouse job near our new place, so we might be able to afford something better soon, or at least afford to survive until he gets something better. I'm just ready to move on and start over. I'm hopeful that this school will be a better fit for me, and I just hope that Shawn can deal with not being the most popular guy in school this time. The neighborhood we're living in is closer to what dad calls the projects. He said it's near where he grew up. P.S. 22 West is the high school that he attended when he was younger. He said that when he went there, it was a primarily black school. That's probably the most significant change for us and the most exciting for me. At the very least, I won't be a target for anyone just because I'm black.

The few things I have left to pack are still sitting at the end of my bed to finish in the morning. I venture down the hall to see if Shawn is holding up. His door is wide open, and he is sitting on the floor, unloading his clothes from the bottom drawer of his dresser. I gently knock on the door frame to get his attention. "You doing ok, man?" I ask him, knowing that the answer is no.

"I'm alright, I guess; This sucks, though. I don't want to have to move into the city.

From all of the stories that dad has told us, it's going to be a nightmare." I knew Shawn was having a rough time dealing with the transition.

"Well, how was school yesterday?" I asked.

"It was fine. Saying goodbye to everyone was weird. Everybody is still pissed at you—" "Good!" I couldn't help but interrupt. "I'm glad to be leaving those people behind. Moving is going to be good for us, dude. You'll find tons of new friends and be just as popular at this school, I promise."

"I hope so. I don't want to be the odd man out. Sorry," My brother looked up at me, knowing that I know exactly how it feels being the odd man out. "I didn't mean anything by that."

"It's ok. I'm just ready for a new start. Dad should be back any minute with the moving truck." Shawn shrugged his shoulders. I left him to pack the rest of his things. I had to throw the last of my comic books in a box. I put it in the driveway with the rest of our packages and furniture.

Dad and Shawn loaded the bulk of our belongings into the truck while mom and I took the van to see the new place. Driving through the city was different. I mean, I've seen the city before. We've gone through the same neighborhoods thousands of times, but it's like looking through a different set of eyes when you know you're moving to a place that you're going to live. It didn't look like where I belonged, but that's what it was-My home. This particular complex was a building off of 8th & Main. It's not exactly in the worst part of the city, but far from the suburb, we've found ourselves up to this point.

Mom and I pulled up to the building, a high rise of what looked like at least seven stories. It was an old brownstone building, probably built in the twenties. There were bars on the windows of the three lowest floors. Around the front of the building was a fence with a gate and call box to get in. We parked in the parking lot adjacent to the tall building, walked up to the call box, and rang the office.

"How can I help you?" A deep voice boomed from the box.

"We're here to move in today. Apartment 303." The box buzzed a three-second-long buzz, and then the gate snapped open. The sidewalk to the door was overgrown and broken, with weeds running through the cracks. An overweight older man greeted us at the building's front door and said he was the superintendent of the building. He gave mom his number if we needed anything, taught us how to use the call box, and handed her the keys.

We took a sharp left inside the door and waited for the next elevator to our new oasis of a living situation. "Mom, on the way here, I don't think I saw us pass one supermarket or department store. Where are we going to buy food? I saw like twenty gas stations and liquor stores between home—uh—our old house, and here."

"I don't know, Drew. We'll have to figure it out when the time comes." Classic response from her.

The elevator opened, and we entered. I pushed the "Three," and we were off. The elevator smelled kind of like a dead animal with the scent of someone that had smoked a few packs of cigarettes in it. I just sighed and held my breath until we got to the fifth floor. Our apartment was 303, just six doors down from the elevators. Good to know if I needed to escape in the middle of the night. We jammed the key inside the doorknob, turned it counter-clockwise, and opened the door to our new palace. When I set my sights on where we'd be living for the foreseeable future, I was all but impressed. The living room was the size of my old bedroom, and the bedroom Shawn and I were supposed to share, the size of a closet, which would be interesting.

"Drew, can you run down to the van and get the few boxes we brought while I go through this checklist and make sure everything works?"

"Yeah, sure, mom." I'd have done just about anything to get out of there.

After an entire afternoon of carrying boxes up and down a buckling sidewalk and loading them into the elevator to send up or carrying them up the stairs, we ordered a pizza. After dad and Shawn returned the moving truck, we spent the evening eating pizza on the floor of a heavily used, barely clean apartment, mostly in silence. If this was a sign of what was to come, we're in bad shape.

The days after the move turned into weeks. We were all learning how to live this new lifestyle that we've become accustomed to being our new normal. We drive thirty or so miles back to our old neighborhood once a week to get groceries. Shawn and I ride the public bus to get to school, which is twelve blocks away from the building. Dad got the warehouse job where he had interviewed. It doesn't pay much, but we're able to get by for now. Shawn has a part-time job working as a dishwasher at a local restaurant just across from the apartment. He volunteered to work there just to help mom and dad with the bills.

Our new school is primarily black. They don't offer any extracurricular classes except one elementary fundamental art class. Football season is over for Shawn, and he doesn't want to try out for any other team. It's not the best situation, but it has been tolerable for the last couple of weeks.

Shawn and I have to wake up an hour earlier just to be able to catch the city bus with enough time to get to school. Shawn barely wakes up on time anymore. I'm always the first one up, flipping on the fluorescent lights to wake him. This morning is no different. His alarm goes off at 6:20 A.M., and he sleeps through it. I crawl out of bed, slap the snooze button, and head off to the bathroom to shower. The bathroom is just as cramped as every other room, but it could be worse. I take a short shower, leaving enough time and hot water for Shawn to get in and out before we have to leave. We scrounge up whatever breakfast we can eat on the go and head out the door and down the stairs. It turns out the elevator only works a few days out of the month, so we've opted to take the stairs every morning instead of waiting to see if today is the day the elevator will be operational. There's always the same older maintenance man down in the lobby working on something or just sitting behind the desk. He's an older black man with salty white hair. His name tag says 'Jimmy,' but we never bother to ask. On today's trip down, he was working on one of the glass entrance doors that had a missing handle. "Have a good one, fellas!" It was always the same line each morning, and in unison, we would yell out, "thanks!" before bolting to the bus stop.

The bus ride takes just over a half-hour to get us within shooting distance of the school. It's still another fifteen-minute walk to get there. We take the same bus home, and it takes even longer with traffic. This school isn't much better for both of us, but it's much worse than it used to be for Shawn. Every morning when we enter the front doors, there's a group of guys that give us shit.

"White Boys!" If you can believe it, we get a lot of heat now for being too "white." There are only a few white kids in this school, and even they don't get as much hate as we do. I'm used to being treated like garbage at school, but Shawn can't handle it as well as I can. He's been getting into more and more trouble, and last week he was suspended for trying to fight one of the guys. He was out for the previous few days of the week, and in those few days, they started to lay into me. I don't know what I'm doing wrong to be "too white," but they haven't let up since Shawn tried to fight one of them.

Darrell is the 'leader' of the group of guys that get onto us every day. This morning he's waiting in front of the school for us. "Hey, white bread is back! Welcome back, white bread!" Darrell is the equivalent of what Jake used to be, except a little more tolerable. Shawn ignores him until it gets under his skin, and he can't go any longer.

"Leave us alone, Darrell. We aren't white. Your jokes aren't funny." I can sense that Shawn is starting to get a little upset again.

"Darrell, just leave him alone. If you want to pick on anyone, pick on me. We haven't done anything to you. Just leave." I try to intercept the heat that Shawn gets. I don't want him to get in any more trouble than he has to.

"You two might as well be white! The way you talk, the way you walk. You just reek privilege. Why don't you go back to the hills where you came from?" barked Darrell.

Shawn grabbed me by the arm and ushered me down the hall. His approach is to get as far away from them as he can.

Darrell's voice got further and further into the distance, but I could still hear him taunting, "That's it! Run, white boys. RUN!".

We got to the end of the hall, and Shawn stopped me. "Look, neither of us needs to be getting into any more trouble. I've already tried to fight these guys once because they pissed me off. You've already been expelled from the last school; We need to keep ignoring them and get through the rest of this semester. Then we don't have to worry about it anymore. Got it?" "I got it, but what's going to happen if they get under your skin again, Shawn? You'll be the one expelled this time. I'm not going to let them do that to you."

"Just stop, Drew. Just stop." Shawn sprinted off to his first class before the bell rang, and I just took a second to gather my thoughts in the hall. We've been here for just a few weeks now, and these guys haven't let up since we got here. I know I have to get the upper hand and let them know that they can't keep doing this. I can't be the same guy I was at the last school. The one who is always afraid, who just sits there and takes the torture. Not again.

My first class was an American History class. History is probably the most boring subject, but Darrell and his gang are in the same class as me, unfortunately. They're always throwing something at my head or trying to trip me when I have to walk past them. Most days, I can get through without injury. It's just like Jake and his goons in Spanish class. I'm tired of laying low and just trying to 'get by,' though. It didn't work for me with Jake, and I doubt it's going to work for me here. The part of it that's bullshit is that I used to get tortured for being black before, and now somehow, I'm being targeted for not being black enough. None of it makes any sense to me.

The days drag by here, and it seems like an eternity to get to the end of the school day, let alone the hour bus ride home. The only other time we see Darrell and his guys is at the end of the day when we're trying to leave to catch the bus. It's been such a sure-fire occurrence that Shawn and I have found a way out of the school's back door. It adds another block onto our trek, but it's worth not having to deal with them harassing us. We sneak down the rear hallway stair that only the janitors use, and what we thought used to be a dead-end turned into an emergency exit door that had been left disarmed. We noticed the wires were taken out of the door handle one day and used this route to get away from the guys every day since. Darrell must've caught on because he was there on the other side of the exit door waiting for us today.

"You boys think you can get away from us that easy, huh?" he said while his friends laughed behind him in unison.

"Look," Shawn said sternly. "What is your problem with us? Why are you treating us this way?"

"We don't like fresh meat around here, and you guys are the whitest niggas we've ever seen here. What's with that? Are you adopted or some shit?"

"For the last time, we aren't white. We're not doing anything wrong." Shawn raised his voice and got a little too close to Darrell for my comfort. "Leave. Us. Alone."

"Or what, white bread. What are you and your gay ass little brother going to do?"

I could see the fire in Shawn's eyes. His fists clenched, and he drew back his right arm. I tried to grab him before he did something we'd both regret, but I saw the anger in his face turn to fear, and when I followed his stare, I saw, in the waistband of Darrell's jeans, a handgun. He had lifted his shirt before Shawn had the chance to land a punch, revealing a small black revolver.

"You don't want to do that, blood" Darrell said to Shawn, with the coldest look. "You'll both regret it. Do you want to die, white bread?"

Shawn grabbed my arm, and we took off in the opposite direction. We ran so fast, and without thinking that we ended up two blocks out of the way, missing the bus, we were trying to catch. We had to walk home, but I was so shaken up that I almost would've preferred to run the rest of the way. "Dude, what is wrong with that guy? A gun?" I tried to get something out of Shawn, but no matter what I said, he didn't have a response. The confrontation with Darrell must've rattled him more than I thought. We finished the walk to the apartment in silence, and when we got off the elevator and through the front door, Shawn went directly to the room and went to bed.

"What do I do?" I thought to myself. "Should I tell someone? Mom? Dad? Should I just call the police?" Talking to someone didn't work before when something like this happened. I can't see Shawn rattled like that anymore. I'm going to have to do something on my own.

Shawn slept from the moment we got home that afternoon, through the night until the following day. When he woke up, he seemed different, still shaken by what happened the day before. He barely spoke the entire way to school the next morning. I didn't pressure him, but I couldn't stand it anymore once we stepped off the bus.

"Shawn, are you ok? You haven't said a word to me since yesterday." He looked me in the eye, clearly distraught.

"I can't stand it here. I want to go back." That's all he could get out. I knew there was more, and I understood what he was saying. As bad as it was before, I'd give just about anything to go back. I couldn't stay seeing him upset, and I knew most of it was my fault. Maybe if I didn't play that prank, we would've been able to make ends meet and stay where we were. If I didn't get expelled, there wouldn't be an extra incentive to have to move. I didn't want to be here anymore than Shawn did, and I couldn't help but think that part of this, if not all of it, was my fault. This place was hell, and we both wanted out.

Not noticing how far we had gotten, I looked up and realized that we were almost to the school's doors, and I could see Darrell waiting for both of us out front. The closer we got, the more impatient I could tell he was becoming. Darrell and his group came up to us at the edge of the school's property. Darrell walked up to Shawn, looking him dead in the eye. I could see that Shawn didn't know what to do or what to say. He was afraid, just like me, and I'd never seen him like that.

"Well, look who's back. I didn't think you boys would come back after running off so scared yesterday!" The group erupted in laughter.

I had to step up. I couldn't lead Shawn into the fate that I'd always accepted. He wasn't weak like me, he didn't get made fun of like me, and I couldn't let it start for him now. "Darrell, we aren't scared of you. Just back off and leave us alone!" I managed to get that out confidently, but I don't know where it came from or how I could say it. Shawn turned his head slowly and looked at me like I had gone utterly insane.

"Oh yeah? What if I don't?" Darrell moved toward me and was about an inch from my face at this point. I don't know what came over me, but I could feel the fire rising inside me. I took one deep breath, quite possibly my last, looked at Shawn, then down at the back of my hands. They were trembling. I knew what I had to do to defend my brother.

I looked Darrell right in the eye and said, "This." I swung my left fist with all my might and clocked him straight in the nose. He fell to the ground, blood pouring from his face. The next thing I knew, all three of his goons had jumped on top of me and started pounding their fists into my chest and face. It was excruciating, but I had gotten so tired of playing the victim. I didn't want Shawn to start feeling the same way. I tried kicking them all off of me with my might, but they kept hitting. It felt like all of the bones in my body were shattering all at once. I could see Shawn trying to fight his way through to help me, but at this point, there was a crowd forming around us, and there were a few guys beside him that were holding him back. There's no sense in fighting back anymore. Any hope I had hung onto up until that point was going. The goons were pulled off me by a figure that I could only see with the eye that hadn't yet swollen shut. The figure stood over me, and the closer they got, the easier I could make them out. It was Darrell, and in his hand was the gun he kept in his waistband, pointed directly at my skull. "This is it for me; This is the end." I thought.

"You messed with the wrong blood, white bread."

I closed my eyes, convinced that I wasn't going to make it out of this alive.

I peeled both of my eyes open. It felt like the skin was ripping off both sides of my eyelids. It stung worse than any pain I've felt before. I could feel a stinging along both sides of my body and in both hands. I couldn't get my eyes open more than a quarter of the way. I don't know where I was, what happened, or if I was even still alive. Had I been shot? Was Shawn ok? Then I heard it, Shawn's voice: "He's awake! Mom! Look," I tried to speak, but nothing came out at first. I could get my eyes open far enough to make out a face that looked vaguely like Shawn's. I pressed my vocal cords to work, but they gasped out an unrecognizable noise. It took more than a few tries to get out anything resembling words.

"Shawn? What happened?" I managed to get something out. I'm just glad I could talk to him and just hear his voice again. He proceeded to tell me that Darrell's guys had me pinned down until Darrell got back up and stood over me with the gun pointed at my head. He had madness in his eyes when he got back up. He kicked me repeatedly in the ribs and then cocked the gun aimed at my forehead.

"I swore he was going to shoot you, and it got me so angry and scared. I clocked the guys holding me back and jumped over the ones in my way to tackle Darrell to the ground. The gun went off but didn't hit anyone." He went on to say that the teachers that had witnessed everything came running out to pull all of the guys off to the side until the police could get there. They were all arrested and taken into custody. "I sat there with you the entire time, just waiting for the ambulance to come. You were barely breathing, and I was hysterical. I didn't know if you were going to make it, Drew. We got here, and they took you back into a room. I couldn't get a hold of mom or dad until a few hours later. That was a couple of days ago. You've been out of it ever since, until now."

"Am I ok? Is anything broken?"

"Your face is pretty mangled, but it'll heal. Your eyes are swollen and bruised, and the doctor said you have two broken ribs. You're looking pretty rough, but you'll pull through. I'm just glad you're still here, brother."

"That makes one of us," I said before closing my eyes again to rest. My brain was racing at this point. What did I do to deserve pain like this? I don't want to live like this anymore. Anywhere I go, pain follows. I've done nothing but struggle. No matter what school I'm at or where I go, I get tortured by bullies. This time it almost killed me. Maybe it would've been better if Darrell had shot me. At least I wouldn't be in pain anymore. My parents don't care about what I'm going through. The only reason they're here right now is that Shawn made them come. I'm sure they have more important things to be doing anyway.

That's it. I'm going to make a plan here and now to finally get out of this cycle. I've had more than enough. I want out. The next couple of days I spent alone in a hospital bed. Mom and Dad were both working, and the distance from our apartment to the hospital was too far for Shawn to walk, so he stayed home. Being alone gave me time to come up with a plan to end it all. All the suffering, all the torture. Everything.

I knew that mom kept a bottle of pain medications in the medicine cabinet at home. I had seen them before. I vowed to myself that as soon as I could get up from this bed and go home, I was going to steal the bottle of pills from the cabinet and head up to the roof of the apartment building.

I didn't want Shawn to have to find me in bed or the bathroom, so the apartment roof would have to do. A stranger may stumble onto my dead body, but it wouldn't be nearly as traumatizing for them as it would for someone in my family. I'd sit down on the rooftop, write a note to mom, dad, and Shawn explaining why it had to end this way, then swallow what's left of that bottle of pills. I'd lay down, let the sunshine pour over my skin. I'd feel the heat beaming off my face and slowly slip away and out of this horrific cycle that I'm stuck in for eternity. It was a fool-proof plan. There's nothing that could go wrong. I'd finally be free of the pain that I've felt for so long—no more bullying. No more almost getting shot for being "too white." No more having the life kicked out of me for being black. It would be over.

They brought in a psychologist the next day to evaluate my mental state after "such a traumatic experience." The doctors assured me that it was just a routine procedure to bring someone in for an evaluation and that I had no reason to be concerned. The psychologist entered my room later that afternoon. He was a tall, thin black man who was surprisingly easy to talk to.

"Hi Drew, I'm Dr. Mindel, but a lot of my patients call me Dr. Mind. I've been sent here by your doctors to ask you a few questions and make sure you're doing alright. Does that sound ok?"

"Yeah, that's fine," I said reluctantly.

He asked me some routine questions about my mental health history and some basic questions about me. He seemed nice enough, but I had already made up my mind. No therapist could talk me out of finally freeing myself of all of the torture I've been through in this life.

"The doctors have told me all about what happened to you. I'm sorry you had to go through that. Is there anything you'd like to talk about with me?"

I rolled my eyes, "I'm bullied a lot. This week was only the third week I had been at this school, and I was almost killed by some kid who thought I was acting too white. I don't know what I keep doing wrong to deserve to be bullied so much."

"How's your home life, Drew? Have you talked to your parents about what's going on?" The doctor asked.

"I learned a long time ago not to bother. My parents don't care."

"What makes you think that they don't care?" Dr. Mind asked.

"I don't just think that they don't care. I know it. I've been through all of this with my parents before. I've tried to confide in them, but they either stop listening to me or tell me to suck it up and get over it. I'm not like them. I didn't grow up surrounded by trauma, but I don't always need to be told to suck it up or that I am too soft. I should be listened to and helped, especially by my parents. I don't know what's wrong with them." I don't know why I let all of that slip out, but it felt good to get it off my chest finally.

"Well," said the doctor, "You have quite a strong opinion on the subject. Have you ever thought about seeking out someone else to talk to, like a therapist?"

"My parents would never let me. They don't think it's necessary." I mumbled back.

"Do you think it's necessary for yourself, Drew?"

I thought about it, and it would be nice to have someone to talk to about these things. "Yes, I guess it does seem that way."

The doctor finished filling out the notes he'd been scribbling down as we spoke, shut his notebook, and walked to the foot of the bed. "I'll discuss everything with your parents when they're in next, and we'll see if we can get you some help."

"Thanks, Dr. Mind." I guess the guy was alright. It did feel kind of nice to get those things off my chest.

I didn't see Dr. Mind again for another three days. I was just about to be released, and my parents came with Shawn to pick me up to head home. My parents were signing the release papers when Dr. Mind entered the room. Before pulling my parents aside and giving them some insight into the conversation we had a few days prior, he waved to me. He handed them a card along with a few papers and left the room.

Chapter 6: Dr. Mind

My parents have been on the fence about me starting therapy with Dr. Mind. They've been thinking it over for over a week now. We're supposed to sit down and talk about it tonight before making a final decision. Coming home from the hospital wasn't easy, and I'm still unable to go back to school for another couple of weeks. My parents pulled Shawn out for the same amount of time so that he could be home to help while I heal. They can't afford to stay home with me, especially not with the possibility of paying for therapy on the horizon.

After dinner, my parents sat me down while Shawn was in the kitchen cleaning up. They finally wanted to discuss therapy with me, but I wasn't hopeful that they'd care enough to let me see Dr. Mind regularly.

"Drew, it's going to be hard to stay afloat if we have to pay for you to go to therapy with Dr. Mindel. It's hard enough to keep up as it is." Dad was always straight to the point with things like this. No time for any flowery details.

"I understand, but I think it would be good for me to go into therapy right now. It's been a hard year, and if I don't start to figure some of this stuff out, it's only going to get harder." The more I thought about it, the more I was convinced that there could be another way out of the cycle—something besides ending my life. I could see myself in therapy.

"Drew, I don't think it's a good idea. Your father and I went through a lot, just like you are, and we never had to get therapy. It's too expensive and unnecessary." I never thought mom could make dad look like the good guy.

We were all stunned when Shawn came barreling around the corner to confront everyone. He came in like a bull around the corner from our bedroom, interrupting the conversation.

"You guys are more selfish than I thought if you're going to keep him out of therapy just because it's too expensive for you. It's his mental health on the line. I know you both think you're too strong for therapy, but you'd probably be able to understand both of us better if you had some capability to talk about your feelings."

"Shaw—"

Before mom could stop him, Shawn continued in my defense. "Drew is a good kid, and he's been through a hell of a lot more than both of you. Why can't you see that? Drew was bullied every day for the last two years. Neither of you has been there to see him suffer. You're always working or sleeping. You're never there when he needs you or when I need you. All we have had lately is each other, and until recently, I was too worried about my ego to be there for him. The least we could all do for him is give him some way to understand why he's feeling the way he is. If you're worried about the cost, I can take on more hours at the restaurant, and I'll pay for it. We all owe Drew at least that."

Mom and Dad were silent, and I was so stunned I couldn't speak either. Shawn turned around and went back to washing dishes. My parents looked at each other, and I could see them mentally trying to make it work for the first time I could remember. The conversation ended there, and they set me up to begin therapy with Dr. Mind the following week. My parents called Dr. Mindel's office to set up the appointments. Individual treatment was once a week. Dr. Mind suggested that I attend his local therapy group for teens. Dr. Mind held it just a few blocks from our apartment, and my parents agreed. I could see a way out of this. I just hoped that therapy would work.

It all started with one-on-one therapy with Dr. Mind once every week and group therapy on the weekends. A group of about twelve kids, all around my age, all went through similar situations. We talked about what we were going through, shared our stories, dreams, and aspirations. One-on-one therapy was once a week on Wednesdays. I'd have to take the city bus at 5:15 A.M. to get to Dr. Mind's office by 8:30 A.M. Shawn would come with me every morning to make sure I got there safely. I knew he'd rather be there than back at school anyway. Dr. Mind's office was in a safer part of the city. There were new developments everywhere and skyscrapers on the corner of every block. It was such a lovely area that I felt like I didn't belong—a typical feeling for me at this point. Shawn and I would get off at the bus stop right across from the office building. Sometimes we would sit there and look at the city in awe at all the people coexisting, rushing to work or rushing to get a coffee. It was a hectic but peaceful feeling watching those people. Dr. Mind's office was on the tenth floor of the building. Shawn waited for me in the lobby of the office, but he didn't mind. The receptionist always offered him soda and snacks. I think he had a thing for her. I laughed every time he would shyly say yes. His face turned bright red like clockwork. Those few moments have been the lightest in my life lately.

Mind's office was warm and inviting. Upon entering, you were immediately surrounded by bookshelves. There must've been thousands of books there. Dr. Mind's desk was a giant command center in the middle of the room. A big, bulky, dark oak desk with gadgets on top, some children's toys. For the patients, there was a comfortable leather chair parked in front of his desk. It wasn't that comfortable, but it didn't matter to me.

"Mind?" He didn't mind that nickname.

"Yeah, Drew?" He was standing at one of the bookshelves hunting for a notebook.

"What are all of these kid's toys for?"

"I work with a lot of children, a lot of displaced children in the system. For some, it's the only outlet they have to play with a toy or forget what's happening in their lives. They're a comfort for them."

"You mean kids younger than me need therapy?" I asked, truly curious.

"Well, of course. The sooner someone starts therapy, especially if that person experienced trauma at a young age, the sooner they're able to develop healthy coping mechanisms."

The fact that kids younger than me are getting therapy is comforting to me and a scary thought. I know people go through traumatic events, and it's not dependent on age, but it saddens me that younger children would have to feel the way I've been feeling, or worse. I couldn't imagine being strong enough to go through what I've been through at a younger age.

"I'm glad you're here for those kids, Mind."

Dr. Mind found the notebook he was looking for and looked up at me. "Well, thanks, Drew, but let's focus on you for now. You've been out of the hospital, what, almost a month now? Today's session is our third session. How do you feel about therapy? What questions do you have?"

"I like group therapy. There are a few kids from my school that I even recognize. That one girl, Jessica, or Jazzy, I think that's what her nickname is. Anyway, we've gotten to talk a bit during the exercises we do, and I like her a lot. She's so interesting. She's funny. She's smart, and she's incredible. Especially after hearing what she's gone through. Her parents left her abandoned, her living with her grandma, and their financial struggles. It just makes me happy that people like her can find help and better their lives."

"That's admirable of you, Drew. You are thinking so much of other people. You're very intuitive and very caring. What else are you getting out of therapy? Are you learning anything about yourself?" Dr. Mind knows how to pry with his questions.

"I mean, yeah. I guess I'm learning that I do care a lot about other people. My family hasn't always been the type to show any affection, and I guess that's part of why I felt like such an outsider. I always turned to food to cope, and that just heightened my problems. I got made fun of so much for being overweight, being black, or just being different. I guess I can see now that being different isn't a bad thing. I just have to keep working on myself and being confident in myself. I can see how confident Jazzy is in herself, and it sort of rubs off on me, I guess."

"I paired you two up for a reason, Drew. I think you have a lot to teach each other, and I'm excited about the next group therapy. You're learning a lot about yourself, and I'm proud of you."

He said he's proud of me? I don't think I've heard those words from anyone before. I sat in that leather chair in front of his desk without an expression on my face. I never thought I could make anyone proud before, but Dr. Mind just said it flat out. Nobody has been proud of me, and nobody has made me feel the way Dr. Mind has in these sessions. Maybe therapy will be the thing that works for me.

It took a few seconds before I could respond. "Mind, what makes people not able to say something like that? What makes them unable to say that they're proud of someone or that they care for someone? I've never heard that from my parents before, or anyone, but you just said it without hesitating."

"Drew, it's true. I am very proud of you. Some people don't have the tools to navigate their emotional landscape. You can't hold it against your parents; you'll only grow to resent them.

What we can do is get them in for a session, or if that's not an option, you can work with them on your own. Just be very open about your feelings and have honest discussions about the things you need to hear from them. I can give you a few exercises to work on with them. Everyone is in control of their emotional maturity. Some people just have a longer journey than others, and there's no shame in that."

"Thanks, Mind." I shuddered at the thought of trying to work with my parents on their emotional issues, but if it's what had to be done to feel the way I just felt when Mind said he was proud of me, then I'd do it.

"You're back to school in just over a week, right? Is there anything you're concerned about with that?"

"School has always been rough for me. I've been made fun of, just like I told you. I guess my parents received a call from our principal a few days ago saying that the four guys involved in our fight had been expelled and that the school had placed restraining orders on all of them. They can't come within a few city blocks of the school. My parents decided not to press charges on Darrell, which is fine. I just hope he finds some kind of help. I'm nervous about going back to school, but I think I'll do fine. At least I have a group and these sessions if something happens, you know?"

"Exactly, Drew. We're always here." Dr. Mind was so incredible. I didn't think anyone believed in me or supported me until these sessions started. "Listen, the group therapy is on Friday. Same time. Same place. The community center is just a few blocks from your house, right?"

"Yeah, I'll be there. It's still at 5:30, right?"

"Yes, sir. 5:30 sharp."

"Hey, Mind, if I can convince him to, can my brother Shawn come with me? He usually has a shift on Friday nights, but he's off this week. He's been the biggest help to me in getting therapy. I just want him to see what it's like."

"The more, the merrier. The group is open to anyone that can join. We'd be more than happy to have Shawn."

"Thanks, Mind! I'll see you Friday night."

"See you then!"

I jumped up from the chair I'd been seated in for the past forty-five minutes, practically running out of the office. I stopped midway when I realized my leg had fallen asleep and my ribs were still healing. Walking into the office lobby, I could see Shawn leaning over the receptionist's desk in a trance while she talked.

I couldn't help but laugh out loud. "Come on, sprung boy. Let's go." I grabbed his arm, and he stumbled backward, making sure to wave goodbye to his new girlfriend. We got into the elevator to head down, but Shawn was still looking back at the receptionist. It wasn't until the door opened and I pulled him through the elevator doors that he broke out of his trance.

"I like your therapy days, dude." He glowed. It was nice to see him get that back finally.

"No, you like that receptionist!" We both laughed out loud the entire trip down. The elevator buzzed, and the doors popped open on the main level of the building. "Let's go," I said. We walked out of the building and started our trip to the bus stop to catch our ride back home.

On the bus ride home, I decided to ask Shawn about the group session. "Hey, I was talking to Dr. Mind about the group session this week. I know you have the day off, so I asked if you could come to sit in on a session with us."

"I don't know, man. I'm not good at emotional stuff." It's true. None of us were.

"That's exactly why I'm asking you to come. Look, mom and dad aren't that great at helping us, and I've seen you struggle since we moved out here. I know you're going through it just like I am, and I thought it might be nice for you to have some way to get it all out. Therapy has been such an incredible help for me. I'm losing some weight; I can better manage some of the things I couldn't even think about before and look at us. We're laughing again. Come on, Shawn, please come."

"I'll think about it, dude." Shawn turned his head to look out the window at the passing cars. I hope he comes around by Friday.

The next forty-eight hours went by in anticipation of group therapy. Shawn and I haven't talked about it since the bus ride home from Dr. Mind's office, and I still don't know how he feels about it.

"Drew, come here!" I could hear my mom's voices from the living room through our particle board walls. I wonder what she could want and why she's home so early.

"Coming!" I walked into the living room; Shawn followed closely behind. Dad hadn't left for work yet, and I guess mom had just gotten home. "Here we go," I thought to myself. The last time we were all together because we needed to "talk," it was terrible news. News that ended us up here.

"We want to talk to you about therapy. We can't afford it anymore. Shawn has been nice enough to take on some more work, but it isn't covering the cost of your therapy, and we're drowning in bills. You're going to have to stop your sessions with the doctor. We're sorry."

"No. No, I can't stop going. I'm learning so much that can help us all. I—I just can't quit, you guys. That isn't fair." I was at the point of begging.

"We're sorry, Drew. We can't afford it anymore. This conversation isn't a debate." My father was firm in his demands.

Shawn stepped in again, "I'll work more, you guys. Don't pull him out. He's doing so much better. Just tell me how much more we need, and I'll work as much as I can to help him." Shawn was benefitting too. He had never said such a selfless thing in all the years that I'd known him.

"There's something I have to tell you guys." I reluctantly interrupted, afraid of what I was planning to say next. "When I was in the hospital after the fight, and you guys weren't able to come to see me at all, I felt more alone than I ever have."

"—Son, you know we had to work. We—"

"Let me finish." I'm putting my foot down. They can't keep making these excuses. "I know you had to work to make sure our bills got paid on time and we had food on the table. I get that, but even before we were struggling so much, you guys were still never there for me, or Shawn for that matter. We have only had each other since I could remember. We cooked for ourselves, got ourselves to school, and depended on each other for support. I understand you both had obligations, but this therapy has changed everything for me, and Shawn is coming to the group tonight so he can get some help too." Shawn's eyes turned quickly to meet mine. "I'm not settling anymore. You're coming tonight, Shawn. We both deserve this help, and nobody is taking it away from us. What you guys don't know is that while I was sitting alone in the hospital, feeling like I had nothing left in the world, as though my life would never have the chance to get better, I made a plan to commit suicide." Everyone's eyes fell straight on me. Silence filled the room, and I could see the pain on my mother's face. "I made a plan that when I got back here, I would steal some of the pills from the bathroom and take them all. I didn't want to live with so much pain anymore. I would've done anything to get out of it, and so I made the plan to kill myself. I know it seems selfish to you guys, and before you try to make me feel bad about it, stop. Dr. Mind came into my hospital room for an evaluation, and he just talked to me. Let me talk about my feelings and how this situation made me feel. That was the moment that took away just a little bit of the pain to keep me from boiling over. I kept the plan to myself. I kept it in my back pocket if things didn't get better, but then the group happened. Then the sessions with just me and the doctor. Each one took away a bit more of the pain and helped me deal with what's happening. I've never felt better than I do today, and you guys can feel the same. Dr. Mind has some tools to help us all deal with what we're going through. We can all get out of this cycle."

Shawn stood up from his seat. "We'll make this work no matter what. Drew is NOT quitting therapy." He grabbed my arm and took me back to the room, leaving our parents sitting in shock. "Is that all true, Drew?"

"Yeah, you know what I've been through this year. You know how it has affected me."

"I didn't know it was that bad, man. You could've talked to me."

"I tried, Shawn, but you were just as affected by what happened here, and until we moved here, I couldn't even talk to you. You were caught up in being popular and being liked. I was alone."

"I'll go to a group therapy with you. I want to get help. I want to make sure you get this help. We aren't quitting on you. *I'm* not quitting on you anymore."

Shawn turned to grab his clothes and get ready for our session. I could see tears forming in his

112

eyes while he was talking about getting help. I knew we needed to do this, and I'm glad Shawn can benefit from it too.

We both got changed and ready to head to our group session. We walked out into the living room side by side and saw our mom still sitting in silence, contemplating what had just happened, everything I had said. Dad had already left for work, but I'm sure he went on without being too affected by it.

"We're headed to therapy. Think about what we need to do to keep this going, and I'll ask for more hours at work or get another job. Just tell me what I need to do, mom." Shawn laid it out for our mom once more before we walked out the door. I can't help but be proud of the change that I've seen in Shawn. It makes me happy to know that he's come as far as he has.

Group was just a couple of blocks from the apartment. We arrived about fifteen minutes early. Once I pushed open the community center doors, I could hear Jazzy from down the hall laughing. I couldn't wait for Shawn to meet her. Four doors down on the left-hand side was a mid-sized room carpeted in the ugliest shade of green you'd ever seen. There were four tables with chairs scattered around each of them. Dr. Mind was sitting at the head of the room, and a few people had already arrived.

"Drew!" Jazzy ran up to me and hugged me. I was taken back by the gesture. This moment is the first time she'd embraced me, but she clung so tight that I had no choice but to hug back. "Drew, I've missed you! I haven't seen you since last week. You need to take my phone number so we can finally talk more. She grabbed my phone from my pocket and dialed her number. "There! Now we can talk more! Come on! Sit by me!" She had the energy of a thousand suns and was the most beautiful thing I'd ever seen. I don't know what she saw in me, but I wasn't going to question it.

"Wait, I want you to meet my brother, Shawn." I waved at him to come over. "Shawn, this is Jazzy, the girl I was telling you about."

"Oh, you were telling him about me, huh?" She winked at me. "It's nice to meet you, Shawn. Is this your first time here?"

"Uh—" Shawn was visibly overwhelmed. "Y— Yeah. It is. It's nice to meet you."

"Come sit at our table!" Jazzy grabbed my arm and led me to the table, waving Shawn over in our direction.

"What the hell?" Shawn mouthed to me as I looked back. I couldn't help but laugh and shrug my shoulders at him.

Dr. Mind started the session, and soon after, Shawn, Jazzy, and I sat down; the remainder of the group flooded in. "Welcome back to the group, everyone. We're going to pick up where we left off last week, but first, do we have anyone new to the group?"

I elbowed Shawn, and he raised his hand.

"I'm going to take a wild guess and say that you must be Shawn, am I right?" Mind asked.

"Yeah, I'm Drew's brother." He said sheepishly.

"Hey, Shawn!" Everyone said in unison.

"Shawn, luckily, we have an odd number of people tonight. We do a lot of our work in pairs, so you'll be with Jennifer tonight." Jazzy clapped her hands in excitement. Jenny was Jazzy's best friend. They always came together. "Jenny, would you like to join Shawn at his table?"

Jenny got up and started walking to our table. She's short like Jazzy, with soft brown skin, deep brown hair, and eyes. They could be twins if nobody knew they weren't related. Jenny sat down at our table, and Dr. Mind started the session. We went through our exercises as a group, taking turns one by one talking about our struggles and breakthroughs for the week. Shawn was shy at first, but once he became comfortable with the group, he was the loud, funny guy I knew him to be. I glanced over at Shawn and Jenny more than a few times, and I could see the sparkle in both of their eyes. Shawn was fascinated, and Jenny, the same. We broke into our groups and worked on our communications skills. We role-played different situations, went through how to approach difficult communication with our partners, and finally told our partners one thing that we liked and appreciated about them.

I looked at Jazzy and couldn't help but like and appreciate everything about her. "I like your eyes, your smile, the way you're always so positive and excited to see me. I miss you when I'm not here and can't wait for the next time I get to see you. I've only been here a little over a month, and I feel like I've gotten to know you and express so much with you. I appreciate how great of a listener you are and how much you comfort me when I'm going through something." She looked at me like nobody had ever said anything like that to her, and instead of responding, she just grabbed me and hugged me.

"I appreciate you so much, Drew." She didn't let go for a few minutes, at least.

When the group was over, Shawn and I stood up to get ready to leave and said goodbye to the girls.

"Text me or call me, please!" Jazzy looked at me with a sternness in her eyes that said, "you better call me," and there's no way I could've said anything but, "of course!".

Shawn said goodbye to Jenny and started to head to the door.

"See you later, D! It was nice to meet you, Shawn. Get home safe, guys." Dr. Mind called out from the front of the room. I waved and headed out the door. "D," he called me. Nobody had that nickname for me since Pierce. That's how I knew that Mind was a real game-changer in my life. Pierce was the same way. He was the one who believed in me at that school, and Dr. Mind was that for me now. I guess I truly am lucky to have met such amazing people in my life.

"I can see why you like group therapy now," Shawn said, elbowing my side. "That girl seems so far out of your league, but she is crazy for you!"

"Thanks, I think. Jenny seemed to enjoy you too. See, I told you, man. This group is great. Not just for the people you meet, but for what you learn about them and yourself." I said.

"You're right. I did learn a few things that I could use in life, especially with mom and dad. I think I'd like to keep this group thing up if you're cool with me tagging along."

"Of course I am!" I said. "I think it would be best for both of us. Thank you so much for sticking up for me with mom and dad. I can't tell you how much I appreciate all you've done for me in this. If you thought a year ago that we'd be here right now, would you believe it?"

"No, no way," Shawn laughed. "I'm glad we're here, though." Shawn turned to face me, and for the first time that I can remember, hugged me. "I appreciate you so much, man. Thank you."

We turned to face the alley in front of us and began to walk home.

It was a few days until my next session with Dr. Mind, and a few days after that, I would head back to school. I couldn't help but be hopeful for what was to come. Jazzy and I had been talking non-stop for the last few days, and from what I could tell, so had Jenny and Shawn. Jazzy had asked me to meet her for coffee yesterday, and my mom said it would be okay for me to go but to have Shawn go with me. I mentioned that Jazzy would bring along Jenny, and Shawn was more than happy to agree. Jazzy and I shared a table while Shawn and Jenny went across the street to get something to eat before coming back to meet up with us. We talked for what seemed like hours upon hours about everything under the sun. She told me about her life, how her parents left, and what it had been like for her. I shared my story with her-everything from the school I used to go to, the fights, Jake, and everything that had happened since we moved here.

"I didn't know all of that happened to you, Drew! You're so strong for getting through it."

"Me? Strong? Strong is the last thing I felt while going through all of this. I felt at my lowest low, and when I thought it couldn't get any worse, it did. Jazz, I almost tried to kill myself. It was that bad."

Jazzy sat across from me, stunned. She didn't seem to believe me at first.

"Well, you're still here, and I'm so happy that you are!" she said.

Her eyes sparkle in the sunlight coming through the big bay window of the coffee shop. I'd never met anyone like her ever before. She was kind, beautiful, and such a joy to be around. I don't know what she saw in me, but I didn't care because she did see something in me. She was the most beautiful girl I'd ever seen, and she saw something special in me.

Shawn and Jenny walked through the door, and we both turned to see them laughing and holding hands. Jazzy turned to me, winked, and grabbed both of my hands too. It's the happiest I had seen Shawn before and is the most comfortable I had ever been.

It seemed to be the start of a new chapter for both of us.

I had been contemplating the future lately and decided that I wanted to become a therapist like Dr. Mind. He had indeed saved my life and done so much for Shawn and me and other people. I wanted to provide that same type of help to kids my age and younger. Now that I'm able to cope with everything around me, my anxiety has gone down. I know that I'll have to focus on school and my grades, but Jazzy said she'd help me. She's so intelligent and good at every subject. I'll probably need the help, honestly.

"Jazz, do you think I could ever be a therapist like Dr. Mind?" I wanted her opinion more than anything in the world.

"Of course I do, Drew! You'd be so good at it. You're sensitive and so kind. I know you'd be amazing!"

I was relieved that she thought I'd be good at something. Jazzy would be perfect in every way *and* be so supportive of me.

"Thank you. I know it's hard work, and I'll need you there by my side." I winked at her like she always does to me.

"I'm not going anywhere." She said with a wink and smiled right back at me.

I held her hand the entire way back to the bus stop. Shawn and Jenny were a little bit behind us, still talking and laughing. We took the bus back to Jazzy's apartment, the same building where Jenny lived. When it came time to say goodbye, I asked Jazzy if she thought it would be okay to kiss her before heading up to her apartment.

"I've been waiting for you to ask!" She leaned in before she could even get all the words out.

We kissed for a minute, and it was magic. When my eyes opened and we pulled away from each other, I knew I was head over heels for her. She leaned back in and kissed me on the cheek before turning to run to the front door of her apartment.

"Jen, come on!" she yelled, her cheeks still flushed next to the smile across her face.

Jenny let go of Shawn's hand and ran up to the door. They both waved at us and disappeared into the building. Shawn and I headed home on a high that we had never felt before.

Days later, Shawn came with me to see Dr. Mind for my next session. He didn't bother talking with the receptionist this time, though.

He waited downstairs while I went up for my appointment. I took the elevator up to Dr. Mind's floor and headed to his office. The door was already open, so I took it upon myself to go inside. His office always smelled of cedar and pine. It had become something of a comfort. I felt instantly at ease every time I walked in, and today was no different. Dr. Mind was sitting at his desk with his face buried in a thick, leather-bound book. He looked up when he sensed that someone had entered.

"Hey D! How've you been?" Mind said as I shut the heavy office door behind me and took my seat.

"I'm good, Mind. How are you?"

"Great! How did Shawn like the group?"

"He liked it a lot. I think he might've liked Jenny more, though." We both laughed.

"I'm glad he liked it. I have something I wanted to bring up to you guys. Is he here?"

"He's downstairs. Should I get him?" I asked, wondering what he could want with both of us.

"No, I'll call down and have them send him up."

A few minutes later, Shawn walked through the door of Dr. Mind's office.

"Hey, they said you wanted me to come in here to talk for a minute. You okay, Drew?"

"Yeah, I'm good. Dr. Mind wants to talk to both of us." I said.

"You guys, I wanted to talk to both of you because I have a proposition for you. Your parents have been talking to me about feeling overwhelmed by the cost of Drew's therapy, and I wanted to talk it over with both of you before finalizing anything with them."

"Wait, Drew needs this therapy. They can't pull him out. I've been working overtime to help pay for it." Shawn stood up from his seat, clearly heated.

"I think both of you would benefit from this therapy. That's why I've talked to your parents about waiving the cost of ongoing therapy for you both."

Shawn sat back down, and he and I just looked at each other in awe.

"Really? Free, for both of us? Why?" Shawn didn't expect this type of kindness, but I knew Dr. Mind wouldn't give up on either of us.

"You guys are in a unique situation, and my practice specializes in folks who need help covering the cost of therapy. I decided to offer this counseling for free. Your parents accepted when I brought it up to them, but I wanted to be sure to clear it with both of you before moving forward. Shawn, we can schedule your appointments right before or after Drew's, or we can do them together. It's up to both of you. We can get it set up in a bit, but for now, Shawn, if you'd like to wait outside while we finish your brother's session, we'll get you scheduled when we finish."

"Yeah, thank you so much. This gesture means so much to both of us." Shawn had the widest smile on his face. He slapped my shoulder as he left the room.

"Thanks, Mind. I know my brother needs the help just as much as I do. We appreciate this so much." I said, forever grateful to Dr. Mind for being so kind to us.

"It's the least I could do for you guys."

"Mind, I've been thinking lately about the future. I've seen your kindness and how much you do for all of us around you. I've been thinking about what I can do to give back as much as you do."

His eyes lifted from the paper he was writing on, "What do you have in mind, Drew?" he asked.

"I want to become a therapist, like you. I want to work with the kids in this city and help them improve their lives. I have to find a way to help people escape the situation I was in and help people like Jazzy and Shawn. I want to make a difference in the lives around me. If it weren't for you coming into my life, I wouldn't be here right now. You are a superhero in my eyes, and you don't need a cape. Sure, there are fantasy superhero's like *Batman* and *Superman,* but you give our community real hope! Your superhero name should be 'Hopeman'! You truly were a lifesaver, and I'll never be able to pay you back for that. I know there are kids in this city, like me, who are afraid to ask for help or are unsure how to get it. There's not much access to therapy around here, and I want to do everything I can to change that."

"That's admirable, Drew. I can tell you that it'll take a lot of hard work and determination to get to where I've gotten, but if anyone can do it, it's you, Drew." Dr. Mind said, ever encouraging. "I'd be honored to help you get there. We can make a plan once you get back into school. You'll have to buckle down and get good grades. I can help you find a college, look at financial assistance, and enroll. That's what I'm here to do."

"That's so kind of you to do, Mind. I'll work as hard as I need to. Jazzy said she'd help me study, help me get my grades up so I can get into a good college. I don't know how I'll pay for it all, but I can get a job like Shawn. I'll do anything it takes to get there. I want to help kids like me get out of their bad situations. I know you make a huge difference in the lives around you, and I want to be that kind of person." I was determined to do anything to get the chance to be even half of the man Dr. Mind has been for me.

"Dr. Drew Parker. It has a ring to it." Dr. Mind smiled at me with pride in his eyes. "Let's get to work then, shall we?"

To Be Continued